Perry Normal

and

The Moons of Saturn

Mason Stone

To all those who believe. For my Pig, who believes in me.

Disclaimer

This is a work of fiction. All characters and events are fictitious, however they may relate to recorded historical and scientific fact, and are used solely to provide verisimilitude to the story. Any similarity to persons, living or dead, is purely coincidental.

ACT I THE SKY AT NIGHT

ACT II BEYOND THE SKY

ACT III BEYOND BELIEF

4

PART I THE SKY AT NIGHT

CHAPTER ONE THE THIEF

Perry Normal is not an ordinary boy. First of all, he is regarded as a real science genius by everyone at Brackendale Middle School, including Mr. Matson, the head of Science, who has a Ph.D. from Berkeley.

Secondly, he has a passion for astronomy and all things 'space'.

Thirdly, he is the only person in his school who has time-traveled three times. But that's a secret not even his own parents know.

From his backyard, his Celestron Mark VII gives him a perfect view of the Moon, and even a distant peek at Mars. What Perry needed right now was a more powerful telescope. A reflector. Like the one the Science Lab has at school.

It cost $1200 and was a gift from Cornell University, Dept. of Astronomy. No one had access to it except the Science Dept., and the other science teacher was not as friendly as Mr. Matson was.

"No, Perry. This telescope is strictly for supervised use when we are covering the unit on planets and stars. Which won't be until next April."

End of discussion. Mr. Subramanian was very strict, and had been in the department longer than Mr. Matson.

"Steal it!" said Randy, the school's resident troublemaker. In fact, everyone called him 'The Gorilla'. His manners were primitive to non-existent. He annoyed everyone.

"No, *borrow* it," said Robert, Rita, Henry, and Max. 'Borrow' meant take it indefinitely, without permission, and hope it won't be missed by the Science Department, until April anyways.

Fat chance! thought Perry.

But the upcoming conjunction of Jupiter and Venus was something Perry could not miss. Mars was closer to Earth at any time in the last eleven years. The amateur astronomy community was saying they have evidence of a mysterious planetary body beyond Neptune that is pulling our solar system out of the ecliptic plane. This must be investigated!

That is why, one Friday night in October, Perry Normal decided to become a thief.

***

Doors have locks for a reason. Schools have janitors who double as night watchmen, and closed circuit cameras, and door and window alarms. Lots of barriers to any would-be vandals or break-in artists. But honestly. What is there in a school that anyone would break in to get? Most kids avoid being at school, unless they have to be. If you are in the band, or music club, or on a sports team, or have a detention and have to stay after school, then your presence may be required a bit longer.

Some teachers stay late, but rarely until dinner time. Administrators and guidance counselors don't stay past five, if *that* late. After school games or rehearsals end within a reasonable time. By six o'clock, the halls are empty, the change rooms deserted, the music studio silent.

However, there might be the odd occasion when a student or faculty might work later. Often it was the ancient librarian, Miss Ethel Floon. She lived alone, and often worked late doing specific tasks that only librarians did. Re-shelving books dumped on tables. Cataloguing new books, or CD-ROMs, magazines that the school had purchased for purposes of research, or just to promote literacy for an Internet generation.

She had eyes in the back of her head. She could see 360°, and hear a mouse fart. So it was, that Miss Floon thought she heard footsteps on the stairs that go up to the second floor where the Science Lab was, very late one October evening.

The night the 100x Newtonian reflector telescope got up and walked out of Room 204A.

Much later, when the loss was discovered, Miss Floon would report that she was sure she heard footsteps, but was confused about which date that had occurred.

But for now, in early October, the instrument was assumed to be in a cupboard under lock and key, in its black hard shell case with the eyepiece in a small felt bag tucked inside.

The telescope was awkward to carry, but Perry managed to get it to the exit door and out to the walkway, and the darkness of the back field. Henry was waiting.

"Hurry, Perry! If we get caught, we're toast!"

"Grab the other end, Henry. I nearly dropped it on the stairs. The lights in the library are still on, which means Miss Floon is still lurking about. She could have seen me, but I'm sure she didn't."

"Let's get to the gate and the alley, at least." Henry was huffing and his glasses were fogged up.

The gate led to an alley that led to a dimly lit street that led to Henry's house. The plan was to stash the telescope in his basement, and when his parents were asleep, sneak it up to the balcony and set it up, and stargaze all night, if they wanted to.

Under cover of darkness, leaving a trail of footprints in the dew forming on the grass, the two boys entered the basement through a side door at 217 Copernicus Crescent, and stood it in the corner behind the bar in the family room.

"Phase One complete," said Perry.

"We did it! I can't believe we did it!" Henry was excited and super nervous. He took his glasses off and cleaned them, like twenty times.

"My parents are going away to Boston this weekend. We have the whole house to ourselves, Perry."

"Great! I'll tell my Mom that I am going to sleep over."

The weather forecast called for clear skies both nights. There was even the possibility that the Leonid meteor shower might begin earlier in the month than usual.

***

It seemed like an eternity for Friday sundown to arrive. Perry was ready. So was Henry. This was Science the way it should be— raw, exciting, the great Unknown stretching way over your head, beyond Earth, into the mystery of Space.

"Careful, " said Perry. They gingerly lifted the instrument out of its case and hoisted it in place on the stand.

"It's heavy," Henry complained. It was over four feet in length, six when mounted.

"One sec. I have to get the pins on the tube lined up with the holes in the heavy floor mount. I can't...fit it...don't drop it, Henry!"

A tense moment passed as the 40 lb. piece of astronomical hardware finally snapped into position.

"Where's the eyepiece? I can't see the eyepiece!" Perry was frantic. "It should be in the velvet bag, but it's not."

Without the eyepiece, the thing was useless. And all the effort to get it out of the Science Lab office was in vain.

Then, he saw it.

"It's already screwed into the viewing tube. Somebody forgot to dismantle the telescope properly. Must have been a student—Mr. Subramanian would freak if he knew."

Mr. Subramanian would be very upset also if he knew that a $1200 piece of school equipment that he was responsible for, had been spirited away, and was in the hands of two boys obsessed with discovering more stars, planets, and Near-Earth Objects, from the balcony of a nearby residence.

But he didn't.

The night sky, in all its glory, shone above their heads.

"Milky Way," they said simultaneously. The wide band of stars and nebulae swept grandly across the cool northern skies of upper New York state. The 'River of Crystal' the native Iroquois called it. The Indians, too, admired the stars, and must have wondered who or what lived in those vast galactic depths. It was like looking into the sea, except that it was infinite and full of light.

One day, Perry promised himself, he would know more—much more—about all of it.

CHAPTER TWO   THE MOON

"Wow!" Henry exclaimed. "I've never seen the Moon this close—it's blinding. It looks so real!"

"It *is* real," said Perry. "Look for patterns. Then you can see the anomalies. That's what interests *me*."

The boys took turns gazing up at the heavens through the ten-inch Newtonian scope on its Dobsonian mount that gleamed black in the moonlight.

Something moved through the field of view, something fast and glowing.

"Look, Perry. Aw, it's gone." Henry turned to Perry. "What do you think it was? It was real close to the Mare Imbrium, like it was skimming or searching for something."

"Look at the pock-marked surface, Henry. What do you think made all those craters? Meteors. Centuries of impacts have made the Moon's surface look like that. It happened to us on Earth, of course, but erosion over time and vegetation growth has hidden the real story.

Space is a shooting gallery, Henry. It's just a matter of time until an asteroid, rather than a smaller meteor, comes close enough to Earth to be pulled into its orbit, and...WHAM! School will be cancelled that day, I guarantee it."

"Can't we do something about it? Do we just sit here and wait for the crash of a comet or asteroid?"

"Lucky for us, JPL and NASA have programs to track Near-Earth Objects. They patrol the region of the solar system that our orbit around the Sun will pass through. With better telescopes using optical and infrared, they can see lots of things in space we never could before."

"And then what? What if they see some object inbound, or even on a collision course with Earth?"

"That's the sticky part, Henry. We can get some small window of warning to prepare for such a catastrophic event, but we have no means of stopping it, as yet. That is what scientists and engineers worldwide hope to be able to do in the near future. Until then, my friend—cross your fingers!"

Perry was grinning, like this was a kind of cosmic game, and like all games—had both elements of fun and risk. And Perry always liked a challenge.

That was why he considered himself a junior scientist. Science could observe phenomena, work on explaining them, and therefore help Humanity control the world around us—and that included Space.

"It's my turn. Why don't you go in and make us some hot chocolate, Henry? I don't know about yours, but my hands are freezing."

***

There was going to be a problem. Neither of them dare mention their little escapade—borrowing the school telescope, and stashing it at Henry's house for their private exploration of the solar system.

Everyone approved of the idea, but no one would have guessed they actually pulled it off. If word got out, then it would get back to the Science Department, and Mr. Subramanian would have a shit-fit! If Perry's name came up, he could be suspended or even expelled! In any case, sooner or later, the loss would be discovered. Then what?

Perry hadn't worked that part out yet.

After school most days, the gang from Brackendale Middle School trooped over to Center Street to the legendary diner, The Malt Shop. Generations of students had spent carefree hours eating and talking in the restaurant that served good old-fashioned home cooking since 1958. The prices had changed, but the ambience had not. This was a home-away-from-home, where it didn't matter what grade you were in, or what your GPA was. You belonged. You were one of them.

"Perry. I need your help with the science lab, on wave theory," started Margot.

"Yeah, me too," a chorus of voices echoed.

Perry Normal was the resident genius in Science and everyone knew his help was never withheld when it came to homework, assignments and dreaded tests and exams. He was their hero, as well as their friend. No one asked more than was fair, or ethical. No one asked him to help them cheat, or plagiarize on a test or assignment. He wouldn't have done it, and they knew that. Good ol' Perry!

"So how about it?" Robert and Max were generous in their own way, and often paid the bill for their cohort of hungry 7th Graders.

"Sure, yeah, let's put our heads together and see what Mr. Subramanian has decided to torment the class with. There is a written component, of course, and a demonstration component, where you have to have a model that shows the principle of Physics clearly. Has anyone approached him about doing a PowerPoint on this?"

"Wow. That's what we love about you, Perry! You think of stuff nobody thought of." Robert was so excited bits of vanilla shake were flying from his mouth. Everybody put their arm over their face in mock defence.

"How many teams are there?" Perry asked.

"Ummm, maybe five or six,' Rita explained. "He didn't say if we could have three people on a team, or not. He never explains anything properly. I hate teachers like that!"

A rumble of agreement passed through the group.

"Kruschevsky never explains anything, period!" Mike was leaning out from the booth where he and Randy and a couple of their buddies were sitting.

"So true!" Rita said. Heads nodded. Mike paid at the cash, and went out with Randy for a smoke.

"OK, people. I have a plan. Let's meet in the library at lunch Thursday, and I'll explain the whole thing. Bring your Science book."

But what was really in his mind was the weather. If the night sky continued to be clear and cold, stargazing would be much better. The light pollution of a big city was not a factor in a small town like Brackendale, New York. One of the nice things about small towns, Perry decided.

***

As an only child, Henrik Gerrit Schuyler enjoyed virtually unrestricted freedom to do what he pleased, within reason. His parents were descendents of an old Dutch family that had deep roots in the history of New York. They were educated, cultured folk, and proud of their traditions. They realized that Henry was a gifted child with a bright future in Science or Engineering, and were already planning a college for him to attend post-secondary. They were, what Perry's dad—an accountant--called 'old money'. All the wines they like started with a 'C': Chardonnay, Chianti, Cabernet.

So when Henry casually mentioned that the telescope in the family room was on loan from the Brackendale Science Department, his parents never said another word.

Which worked out very well for the boys, who came home from school promptly, so their evenings could be enjoyed on the balcony with an eye on the stars.

Of course, Perry's parents were in full agreement with his sojourning at Henry's. Perry had won first prize at the New York Science Fair last year and was regarded as Brackendale's native son by everyone in town. He made the papers. He made his family very proud, and his future was assured as an up and coming scientist who would do great things. No one doubted that. Perry had a reputation to live up to.

"Let's do Mars tonight, Henry," said Perry.

"Cool! Can we really see it? I mean, close up?"

"We're going to find out in two secs, as soon as I figure out this mount thing. There!"

Perry swung the tube on its pedestal, which was why Dobsonian scopes were easy to use. You could swivel them with whisper smoothness, and point them in any direction.

"Henry. I see it. I see Mars. Here. Look!"

Perry's voice trembled with excitement. He moved aside and let his friend look into the viewing tube.

"There's a big valley or canyon right across the middle of the planet," Henry said.

"That's Valles Marineris, bigger than the Grand Canyon; six times deeper and ten times longer. Scientists can only guess at what caused that tremendous gash. Maybe a collision with something huge and nasty."

"Where's Olympus Mons, the highest volcano in the solar system?"

"West of the canyon, in the Tharsis Uplands. Swing the scope just a hair and it might be visible."

It was. A giant volcano 70% greater than Earth's highest mountain, Mt. Everest, towered over the sand and stone of the fourth planet from the Sun.

"Think about it, Henry. Organizations are already planning to colonize Mars, maybe in our own lifetime. That Dutch group-- Mars One recruited over a thousand applicants for their proposed voyage to Mars in 2022. They have gone through two rounds of selection, taking mostly highly educated and younger people. This started in 2012, and since then, Elon Musk and Richard Branson have pioneered private space vehicles that could conceivably pull it off. NASA is not the only player in the Space Race now."

"Oh man, I would love to be on that ship. That would be totally awesome."

"Let me remind you, Henry, that Space One says this is a one-way trip. We are not at the stage where we can promise to bring you back home again."

"Oh." Henry looked at the ground for a moment. "They'll build a colony and maybe it will be amazing to stay, like the pioneers in the Old West. They never planned to go back to St. Louis, or wherever. They were so courageous. I can't imagine."

"Well, they'd better be right about finding fresh water on Mars. Recent Mars Rover photos show evidence of large water bodies and erosion, and what looks like lakes in different areas of the surface. Without water, life as we know it just can't exist."

"Think of it, Perry! We could maybe go to Mars, like, when we're middle-aged or something. On a shuttle. Maybe by then the rockets will be powerful enough to get us there faster than the six to nine-month journey now."

"Let's do it, Henry. Let's go to space together."

***

It was Thursday. This was the day they would plan how to do the Science assignment on Wave Theory. Perry began by pairing off the small group of best-ever friends: Max and Robert, who would do waves in water, showing the effects of interference on wave patterns. They would make a mock harbour with piers and a breakwater. Margot and Rita and Kate would do waves in sound; they would demonstrate how human hearing occurs, the structure of the ear, and the nature of vibration. They would compare human hearing to that of dogs and bats. Kate wanted to show that dolphins and whales communicate by sound underwater. Charmaine didn't have a partner so she teamed up with Kate as a pair.

Lastly, Henry and Perry would demonstrate how and why a laser works, and how light waves can be used as carriers for electronic data, and compare them to microwaves used for that purpose. And although Mr. Subramanian had not specifically said, they were going to have an audio-visual component that would explain the science behind each and every one.

The library had computers, and print resources of various kinds, so naturally they planned to spend quite a bit of time in there. Miss Floon approved. She wanted the library to be a center for learning, and secretly wrote proposals to the School Board for more funding for more books and software. She asked the principal to allow the library to take over an empty storage room, by knocking down a wall and installing new workstations. Principal Adams said he would talk to the committee at the Board to allocate money for it.

Miss Floon was like that. Always doing something that made her feel useful. She was even doing a Master's degree online, to keep her engaged in what she regarded as her 'calling', like God placed her on Earth to catalogue books.

"Can we use Wikipedia as a reference, Miss Floon?" a student was asking.

"Technically, it is regarded as suspect, weak. Try to find a published book or magazine instead," Miss Floon replied. She also offered tutorials in APA and MLA formatting for research papers and essays. She composed an article to be circulated on the library website and to every teacher, on the topic of Plagiarism, which was her personal bugbear, and proof that Evil existed in the world.

"We'll meet in one week's time, same place," said Perry. "Good luck everybody."

The small band dispersed to grab some lunch before Third Period after lunch, which was either Math or Socials, depending on where you were in the cycle.

"Henry. Henry!" Perry hissed in a low voice so as not to attract the attention of Miss Floon, who forbade chatting of any kind in the library. How were you supposed to communicate with your seatmate? Write notes? Texting? Nope. No cell phones to be in sight in the Library. Rule #12.

"Let's move on from Mars and see if we can see the outer planets," Perry said.

Henry nodded.

"Meet at your house at 7:00."

***

"Henry. There's some technical fix we have to do. Something is wrong with the image we're getting."

"What do you mean 'wrong'?"

Perry continued. "It's way too blurry to see clearly. I read on the Internet that you have to 'collimate' the scope. That means we need to align the primary and secondary mirrors with the eyepiece, so it focuses correctly."

"Easier said than done," replied Henry. "Do we need tools for this?"

"Don't know yet. We have to get the eyepiece lens targeted on the secondary mirror, and then adjust the primary mirror at the bottom of the main tube. There must be adjusting screws that make this possible. We have to do this indoors where there is proper light. And we may have to tweak it once we take it outside, to compensate for temperature variation."

"OK, let's get started," Henry said.

Turns out that very small adjustments involving tiny hex nuts were required to properly align the focal plane. Henry had tools for tinkering with computers and other stuff that were good enough to do the job. Henry had a mechanical talent that Perry was hitherto unaware of.

"Awesome, Henry. Yes, this is much better. I wonder how many amateurs don't know to do this, and think their scope is garbage. All machines need adjustment. Let's take a look for Saturn and its famous rings. That would be amazing if we could see them."

But upper New York State was having one of its famous snowstorms that weekend, and skywatching was out of the question. Perry was frustrated. Henry was disappointed. They had basically two choices: do homework (not great), or play video games (boring). So they decided to surf YouTube for videos on space exploration. This turned out to be a satisfying choice.

"The Cassini Mission revealed much more that we ever knew about Saturn...," the documentary began.

"Cool! We can learn lots of stuff from this, Henry, which will make it more meaningful when we make our own observations. Take notes; this is better than sitting in Science class, and we get to eat and drink and don't have to ask to use the washroom."

"It is still a mystery what formed the rings and why they are separated so precisely and evenly into discrete bands."

"What are those big objects parked in some of the bands?" Perry asked.

"Probably just a camera glitch. Even the Hubble can't give us total clarity of an object over four billion kilometers—that's 886 million miles— from the Sun."

"Say, Henry, you've been doing your homework."

"I *have*. Saturn and its 62 moons get only 1% of the daylight Earth gets from Sol."

"It's incredible that we can see anything out there," Perry said. "Pass the cereal. Got any milk in the fridge? Boy, I hope this storm lasts a week. Then we can really find out what's hot in space news. I love YouTube!"

CHAPTER THREE   ANOTHER MOON

The snowstorm did last longer than expected. It was like a very long weekend for Brackendale Middle School students. Some went skiing and snowboarding, some slept till noon, and some studied Astronomy. Well, at least two of them did.

Henry and Perry were beginning to learn a lot of things about the Solar System. They realized that they was some controversy over various NASA missions, like the Moon landing was possibly faked, or that there was a cover-up about Mars and that maybe there were astronauts already camped out there because the atmosphere was thin but breathable, and so on. Conspiracy theories were common on the Internet. That's why it's the Internet. Just about everybody can post articles and opinions, and many of them probably didn't have a shred of what Perry, the junior scientist, would regard as credible proof or solid facts to back up their claims.

"Still, there must be a reason why people say stuff like that," Henry argued.

"People have come to distrust government and its agencies, Henry. With all the political intrigues and scandals, who can blame them?"

"Yeah, I guess. But my Granddad used to say: 'Where's there's smoke—there's fire.' It seems logical. But how is anyone going to know what really goes on in space?"

"Aha, Henry! That, my boy, is why we...ah...borrowed the school telescope. This is what they call 'primary data', information that we personally collect from our observations. It's just like all the Science experiments we've been learning to design. You start with a hypothesis, develop a method to prove or disprove it, then perform an experiment to gather data to support one view, or the other. That's what amazing about Science, Henry! That's why we are Scientists!"

Perry's voice was getting louder and louder. Like he was giving a speech to the International Astronomical Union annual meeting.

Henry got so excited he clapped. He could hardly sit still.

"Yes, yes, you are right, Perry! We *are* scientists. One day maybe we will make a discovery that will change everything!"

People who are excited often start to eat furiously. The cereal was all gone, so they started on potato chips. Then they raided the fridge for ice cream and anything else that jumped out at them. Scientists need special nourishment, that much was clear.

Once the sky cleared, Perry and Henry were back on the balcony. The frigid air made the stars seem so brilliant and sharp. They had both the Orion and the Celestron out now, for simultaneous viewing. Like spies of the skies, they patrolled the millions of miles of darkness looking for anything unusual. They had some leads from their private research that suggested that many mysteries and enigmas are there to discover.

Perry started a blog to reach out to the skywatcher community. He wanted to start a dialogue with other kids who had the same passion for the wonders of Space.

He joined the American Meteor Society, tracking meteors in space since 1911. He had become a Junior Member of NASA/JPL two summers ago, with the dream of doing an internship at JPL some day. He and Henry both signed up for the Amateur Astronomers Association in New York City.

They found lots of bigger telescopes in the state. The University of Rochester had one. Syracuse had one, and an amazing astronomy club as well. Colgate University Dept. of Physics had one, with the charming name 'Foggy Bottom Observatory'. And of course, Brooklyn had the Edwin Hubble Planetarium. They were certainly not alone in their fascination and love of planets and stars.

"What if we make an important discovery, Perry?" Henry was seated at the smaller scope, a blanket around his shoulders, and his breath smoking in the night air.

"Well I hope we do, Henry! Anything is possible. Many discoveries are made by amateurs, just like us. Comet Shoemaker-Levy 9 was spotted by a guy who spends most nights in the backyard watching, watching; and waiting. It slammed into Jupiter in pieces that would have obliterated New York City, most of New Jersey, and all of Delaware. Who is watching the skies for danger, Henry? That's what I want to know."

Perry returned his gaze to the instrument, scanning beyond the Asteroid Belt for anything that did not look right.

"Hey! Remember the rumors from a couple of years ago about a rogue planet on the outside edge of our solar system? NASA called it Planet X, others called it Planet 9. On YouTube they say it is Niburu, a lost star that burned out, or a huge ghost planet that is incoming on a long elliptical orbit."

"You mean it's one that may be on a collision course with Planet Earth?"

"Yeah. That one," said Perry. "Do you want to try and find it?"

"Totally!!" Henry was easily excited, and when he got excited he babbled uncontrollably. "It's reported to be beyond the Kuiper Belt out past Pluto. One group of conspiracy theorists say it's behind the Sun, ready to slingshot into our orbital path. I don't know. We can find it maybe. Perry, this is what I'm talking about!"

Perry was too concentrated to reply at that precise moment.

"I can't see anything that matches that description, in terms of mass or position," Perry stated.

"But everybody says something large out there is affecting the solar system, so it has to be very big and have substantial gravitational pull," Henry said.

"Then there is something—either they are not talking about it, or they are not sure about it. Henry, maybe we can do something to locate it, if it exists."

"Yeah, Perry. We'll be famous! They will name a high school after us, or something." Henry had continued chattering like a squirrel, non-stop.

Then Perry dropped his cup, breaking off its handle on the deck.

"Henry! Honest to gawd, you won't believe what I saw. Train your scope on Saturn's largest moon—Titan. It appears like a yellowish greenish ball, like a marble or a gumball.

See it? I saw a distinct flash of light quite close to it. What the hell makes a flash of light out there in the darkness of Space so bright that it can be seen from Earth?"

"Not seeing anything, Perry. Looking…
Shit—there it is! There it is, Perry!"

This time Perry was ready.

He mounted his brand new Nikon DSLR to
the view tube and captured two images that would,
in the end, change his entire life.

Chapter Four Room 204A

It was a matter of time, really, till the school telescope would be found missing from Room 204A, the Science Office. Perry and Henry didn't plan to keep it forever, just play with it for a month or two.

It was Monday. Everyone was in a crappy mood because of the bitter winter cold that gripped upstate New York, as well as neighboring Ontario and Quebec. It was great for skiers, hell for drivers. School buses were late, and traffic— even in a small town like Brackendale—was snarled.

First period was Science class with Mr. Matson. He was a teacher with a broad-minded understanding of how the natural world worked, and how good Science helps us interpret that. We all loved him in our own way. That thought was shared by everyone in the gang. But today would not be a good day.

"Let's take a look at how amphibians apparently evolved into land-dwellers," he began. But he was cut off by a racket coming from the Science Office behind him. The other, not-so-popular Science teacher, Mr. Subramanian, was banging around, and shouting.

"Where is the telescope? Where is my fucking telescope?"

Mr. Matson discreetly pulled the door to the lab and classroom shut. But the banging and yelling continued.

It seemed that someone had removed an important piece of equipment without the knowledge or authorization of its owner.

"Mr. Matson? Can I see you for a moment?" The head that poked out the door had a very red face, you could even say it was purple.

"Excuse me for a second. Read p. 169 in pairs and make a brief note. I'll be right back."

Now two voices could be heard coming from the office: one strident and demanding, the other contrite and soothing.

"I'm sure there's a simple explanation, Ravi. Somebody moved it, that's all."

"Moved it to *where*? Without my being told. How do we know it wasn't stolen? I can think of a dozen idiots in the student population who would think that was funny. Well it's NOT!"

The hall door of the office opened and slammed, and heavy footsteps retreated down the stairs.

Everyone in 7E Homeroom had a pretty good idea about what happened to the telescope in question.

Perry and Henry were literally nose down in the book, seemingly plowing through the biological arguments for migration to terrestrial habitats.

The Gorilla had a huge smirk on his face, and was leaned way back in his desk, like he had personally been involved in this amusing (for him) event.

Mr. Matson slipped back into the front of the room. He was pale, although only Margot and Rita noted it.

"Umm. If anyone might know where the school telescope is, please let me know, or give me any clue as to where it is. It weights about 40 pounds and is a big black tube like a pipe, and is, or was, in a black hard shell case. No questions asked. Help me out, people."

Twenty-one students looked at him with innocence written all over their faces.

The lesson continued, but Perry whispered something to Henry, who then nodded.

***

"What now?" asked Henry.

"Simple. We bring it back the way we took it out. Under cover of darkness, after hours.

I still have the Office key, remember? I slipped it into my pocket from Mr. Matson's desk drawer on my way out after he stepped out for a brief meeting with him and a couple of students, and happened to leave the door ajar."

"I wondered how you got in; now I know. OK, when?"

"Tomorrow night. It gets dark around 6pm. We meet by your basement door. I'll tell my parents I'm working late at school, then going to your house to finish it. OK?"

"Got it. Geez, I hope this works. With my luck, Miss Floon will be standing right there, asking: "What are we up to, boys?" with that tone. I hate that."

Perry laughed. "Don't sweat the small stuff, Henry. We got this."

***

They lugged the instrument out the back gate and into the lane. Perry had duct-taped the side door of the school so it wouldn't shut and lock. They made it that far.

Then Henry remembered something.

"Shoot. I left the viewing lens in its velvet bag on the bar. I totally forgot to put it in the case."

"Go back quickly. I'll stay with the scope."

"If they catch you, Perry..."

"Just go. I give you six minutes flat."

Henry was puffing like an asthmatic locomotive when he finally made it back.

"C'mon, Henry. Time is short. The library lights are on, so you-know-who is lurking. What if she's really a wicked witch that catches and cooks unwary students?"

"I wouldn't doubt it," said Henry dubiously.

They mounted the back stairwell that led directly to the second floor Science rooms. Perry slipped the key from his pocket and slid it into the lock. The door swung open with a squeak loud enough to wake the dead.

The glass cabinet was unlocked, as if waiting for the return of its purloined contents. They turned, and very quietly, on tippy toes, slipped out the door into the hall. Again, the door protested the presence of burglars.

And then—the worst moment happened. Miss Floon came into the same hall a few yards down, and turned toward the boys.

"What are we up to, boys?"

Henry's knees started to wobble. Perry thought he might honest-to-gawd faint right there.

"Hi, Miss Floon," Perry said chirpily. "How are you this evening?"

"I heard a squeaky noise out here. Was that you?"

42

"Oh. Sure. We were just getting something from my locker, Miss Floon. We are so busy tonight with our homework that I forgot my...ah...backpack. No. Textbook. Yeah. Those things."

Perry was blowing it. Henry stepped in.

"Hey Perry. Don't forget my parents have dinner on the table. We gotta go!"

"Night, Miss Floon" said Perry as they barreled down the stairs to the exit door and burst into the snow that was coming down like frosty shimmering curtains.

They didn't stop till they reached the end of the lane that opened onto Copernicus Crescent.

Perry fell over in the snow laughing, almost crying.

"We were almost dead meat there, Perry," said Henry. He didn't think it was so funny.

"But we did what we needed to do. Wait till we see Subramanian's face when he sees the telescope in the cabinet. He's gonna have a stroke one of these days."

"What about the key?"

"I'm not dumb, Henry. I put it back in the top drawer of Mr. Matson's desk when we first went in. We're cool. We did it. They should write us up in the school yearbook or something."

"Hey, Henry? Can I stay for dinner?"

***

"Now what do we do? We're effectively blind again, Perry."

Henry was crestfallen, now that the Dobsonian scope was no longer available.

"No worries, Henry. I have a plan."

Perry and Henry met after school at The Malt Shop. Today it was uncharacteristically empty. Maybe it was the weather. Perry wanted to be alone, so it worked out perfectly.

"Let's face it, Henry. The magnification we are looking for requires a massive telescope. Who has such a thing? Well, we'll start with the University of Rochester Department of Physics. I'll write them an e-mail and explain our situation. We are students of Science so I'm sure they will try to help. Besides, it's only a hour or so on the Greyhound, one way. We can get there on our own."

"What we need is a schedule, in case we have to take a day off from school, or something," Henry said.

"What we need is a research plan, Henry. What exactly are we looking for, how will we document what we see, and what will we do with the information once we have it?" Perry looked serious.

Henry also looked serious as he shoved fries dripping with ketchup into his mouth, one after another.

"Like what?"

"I think we are on the same page about this. We are trying to explore—no, *inspect* our solar system for anomalous phenomena—that is, strange and unusual things that don't belong to our current understanding of Space.

Like those flashes, Henry. You saw the photos I took. What the hell was that? What would generate that much energy so far out in the solar system?"

"Volcano!" shouted Henry, exultantly.

"You wish. Of course that is possible if we can assume a molten interior to frozen moons and planets. Or else we have to rethink our definition of 'volcano'. No, I am thinking artificial, something technology-related."

"Like a spaceship?"

"Yes, something like a space ship or space station. Something with metal, and a source of power, controlled by..." Perry hesitated. "By aliens."

"So we are looking for proof of alien life in the Universe?"

"Not exactly. But we must be open to the possibility. What Carl Sagan and Frank Drake believed, what the Roswell Crash started; the investigation must go on. The torch passes to our generation, Henry."

Perry was looking out the window at a blue, blue sky in the bright sunshine, as if he could see into the mystery of Space and Time. The reflection from the snow made it all the brighter. Soon the winter sunset would paint the landscape with orange and pink.

"Look, Henry. There is something happening out there, something that space agencies are keeping very quiet. I feel it in my bones. We have to know. And we have to tell people. Let's go to Rochester. Ask your parents if it's okay if we stay overnight, because I think we need the time. I'll contact the university and arrange to use the observatory during working hours."

"Text me," Henry said, as he paid the cashier.

CHAPTER FIVE   DEEPER AND DEEPER

"These are our people," Perry announced.

"They answered back?" Henry was impressed.

"Yes. There are amazing opportunities there, Henry. What I think we should do is the 'regular' tour of the Mees Observatory. Then, we can connect with ASRAS, which is the leading club for amateur astronomy and they have two incredible scopes for deep sky viewing at night. They meet in a place well outside the city where they can see everything, Henry! This is going to be our big moment. The Mees Tour is this Friday. Let's leave school at noon. What do you say?"

"Let's do this, Perry. How will I get through this week, waiting for Friday to come? That's my problem right now."

However, he was reminded that Science Projects were due next week for presentation in Mr. Subramanian's class. That brought Henry back down to Earth.

For their project, he had gotten hold of a laser pointer that someone at his dad's work had. Henry had constructed a housing to hold it so it would beam directly at a target about four feet away. That part was easy.

It was harder to put together a Powerpoint that debunked the myths of lasers (will it burn a hole if you put your hand in front?) yet revealed the ways that lasers are used in communication technology. Their idea was to point to the future uses in space.

For this, Henry had several slides showing how messages could be bounced off the Moon with lasers and microwaves, and return to the planet virtually instantly.

Perry's slides showed how lasers are carrier waves for other information, such as radio broadcasts or military intelligence. He wanted to avoid making it too complicated and bring in satellites and dishes and relays stations. *Just focus on the science*, he reminded himself.

Wednesday, a bomb threat was received by the school secretary. Everybody had to exit the school as rapidly as possible. The principal was annoyed because State law and school board policy required total evacuation.

This knocked out the whole morning of classes. Mr. Adams knew, as most everyone else did, that this was a hoax designed to mess up the morning tests taking place in Math and Computer Science. Which made Mr. Adams wonder which Math student would be brazen enough to perpetrate such a hoax?

Miss Latimer later confessed that she thought it should be taken seriously.

"I mean, who knows, right?"

That amused the students. Some said because she was Canadian that she was too innocent and easily fooled. "Canadians don't carry guns or blow stuff up, like us Americans". That was Mike's pronouncement at lunch.

Thursday was a previously scheduled fire drill, held for basically the same reasons: school safety and preparedness.

'Another morning shot to hell', someone heard Mr. Adams say in the main lobby, to no one in particular.

So it was that Friday came quicker than Henry had supposed. He signed out at the office at twelve noon sharp, as did Perry.

They sprinted to the local bus that would take them downtown to the Greyhound station. Soon, they were heading west on County Road 104 to the 590 South that went to Rochester. This would take them to the university, and the afternoon tour of the observatory.

Henry and Perry shared a snack of warm pizza and a drink. They were bundled up against the cold. Each had an i-Pod, each with their own audio preferences. It takes very little to make a kid happy. Their parents were very accommodating to them, providing them with every opportunity to learn, and enjoy growing up. They had several hundred in cash between them, as their parents were well-off families living in a very middle class community, with more than its share of post-graduates and highly educated people. They were fortunate, and they knew it.

The tour began promptly. There were retired seniors and veterans, some foreign students, and mostly local enthusiasts who were members of The Astronomy Section of the

Rochester Academy of Science (ASRAS). Perry introduced himself.

"We are 7th graders from Brackendale Middle School, and we want to join and share the equipment and the camaraderie with all of you in ASRAS."

The Planetarium Director was enthusiastic about the group, and welcomed Perry and Henry immediately.

"These are Strasenburgh scopes and are very good for viewing," he said.

Perry learned that they have monthly meetings are can arrange viewing times outside of that, by appointment, and at no charge. Member benefits.

"Hello, Perry, hello,Henry. I'm Bill Barker and this is my wife Mae. We live in Brackendale too, so why don't you come along with us when we attend the club events?"

That was an amazing stroke of good fortune for the boys, and they naturally accepted the kind offer. Besides, their parents would feel much better knowing they traveled safely with local folk.

The tour revealed that there were two observatories: one in Bristol Hills, and the other, the Farash Center for Observational Astronomy, was in another nearby location with excellent dark sky viewing. Perry looked at Henry.

"We came to the right place, Henry, my boy. Look at these telescopes. We can see to the stars in the Milky Way, and beyond. And we don't have to maintain the hardware either."

"Thash tolly awesome," said Henry, munching on chips.

"Please young man," said a lady with a clipboard. "There is to be no food or drink in the observatory area."

Henry blushed and stuffed the crinkly package into his daypack.

"Now we are going to pair everybody off and give you twenty minutes viewing time on the two big scopes here. Make sure you do not touch the viewing tube or lens with your fingers. They require no adjustment—they automatically focus and rotate once the desired target is input on the keyboard. It also compensates for misspelling and simple mistakes like that. Enjoy, and please be aware of the time."

Henry typed 'Proxima Centauri' on the pad, and soundlessly the massive tube moved to focus on the nearest star to Planet Earth. Henry stepped up and put his eye to the eyepiece.

"Oh man! Look! Perry! This is like you are right there; 23 light years just vanishes. Have a peek!"

"Impressive, Henry. This is what we came for, right? My turn next."

Perry typed in 'Saturn Moons and Titan'.

When he stepped down he was pale and trembling.

"I saw it again. Only this time the flash morphed into a large object, drifting slowly toward the rings, on a definite path that indicates intelligent control. Somebody is out there, Henry."

"All right, let's move to the theater," the tour guide said, "where we will show you a short film on the history of solar system missions to date. Right this way, please. Boys?"

The two were staring up at the glittering night through huge panes of glass overlooking the valley, hardly paying attention to the tour anymore.

On the way back with the Barkers, Henry was his usual chatty self; but Perry was quiet, deep in thought.

That night he dreamed of enormous craft drifting slowly over the fields and barns of upstate New York, searching. For what?

***

"Perry, can I speak with you after school today, just for a few minutes?"

Mr. Matson was smiling, and there's no way he would have known about who removed—then replaced—the Department's Dobsonian scope. Perry was curious.

"Sit down, Perry. What I want to talk about is whether you would be interested in a Summer Internship at NASA. Actually, at JPL in Pasadena. They are accepting applications, and although it is usually undergrads and grad students, they do have a few spots for younger students who show promise in Science and Engineering.

They want somebody who can make a contribution to our understanding of Space, and particularly our Solar System. I thought of you! Interested?"

Perry had to sit down for this one.

"Seriously, sir? They would consider me?"

"They require three references from academic or related fields. And you have to write a 300-word essay explaining how this internship would benefit you, in terms of broadening your knowledge of Astronomy and Space Science.

If anybody deserves this chance, it's you, Perry. Mr. Subramanian and I will sign the application, so will Principal Adams, and maybe those people at ASRAS can help with that, too. What do you say? The deadline is in four weeks, so we have to get moving on this."

Perry stood up and shook Mr. Matson's hand. It was then that he noticed how tall he was getting. Gramps was right! He was 'growing like a weed'.

"I will discuss it also with my parents, sir. I am sure they will approve. Wait till I tell Henry! Thank you, sir! See you!"

The next meeting of ASRAS was this Friday night, and the Barkers were going. Perry mentioned that to his Mom, and she was pleased. The Barkers were a bit older and lived on the other side of town, and she mentioned that she should invite them for Sunday dinner sometime.

Then Perry told her the big news.

"Mom, Mr. Matson is inviting me to apply to NASA for a Summer Internship in California. Can I go?"

Lisa Normal was very supportive of Perry and Gabrielle, her two children. In her opinion, they should be given every opportunity to expand their horizons, as she called it, to explore the world outside of a small town in the northern United States.

"It's a big world out there," Robert Normal, Perry's dad, liked to say. "If you want it, you have to go and get it."

"How long is this internship, Perry? Any idea what it will cost?"

Mom made the decisions, but Dad was the accountant in the Normal household. They worked well as a team when it came time to organize things for the family.

"I downloaded the application details; I can show you. I want to ask Jim at ASRAS if he will endorse me. I maybe need another scientist or researcher to sign as well."

Perry was thinking of Professor Wegener at Cornell who was in Astrophysics and had published many respected papers on Space topics. Perry had met him at the state-wide Science Fair over a year ago, and had spoken to him about time-travel and other unusual phenomena. He did not accept Perry's ideas on that subject, but he might still be willing to help get him to JPL.

That would give Perry access to a huge body of resources and data that are available nowhere else in the world.

"Well, whatever you need, dear, we will be behind you. You won't have to miss more than a few days at the end of the school year. Daddy and I will fly down with you. How's that sound?"

"Mom, you are seriously the most amazing mom I could ever have!" He squeezed her hard as they hugged. His dad said how tall he was getting.

Honestly, Perry had not noticed until today, with Mr. Matson, and now hugging his mom. Perry was growing up.

By the deadline, Perry had the references and signatures, the assurance of parental backing, and finished an essay that was somewhat more than the 300-words they asked for. Perry unloaded his sincere and profound feelings—not only about Space study, but his whole philosophy of why Science is the highway to the stars, and how everything in the Universe can be interpreted in terms of scientific laws and principles.

He was afraid maybe he wrote too much; but he decided to let them deal with it. Better to tell them what he was about, than be too vague, and lose the offer of admission.

Six weeks later, they replied. In the offer were documents and forms of all kinds to be completed, signed, and returned. Medical forms, insurance, proof of funding, and on and on. His parents were good at this stuff. It was done, and returned within a week. Perry Normal was going to California!

***

"California?" The whole gang at The Malt Shop was cheering for Perry.

"My auntie and uncle live in the Bay Area," said Robert. "Berkeley."

"Hey, that's where Mr. Matson got his Ph.D.," said Max. "Do you have to be from there to go to university there?"

"Why isn't he called 'Dr.' Matson, then," Rita interjected.

"How long will you be gone, Perry?" Margot wanted to know. They all wanted to know. Their dearest friend and class hero would miss the whole summer vacation.

Actually, they were more concerned that they would miss Perry. His presence was like the glue that held them together, gave them an identity as middle-schoolers. No one wanted to think about what might happen after middle school, or high school, when the winds of Change would scatter them like leaves into the wide world outside.

"C'mon, guys. I'm only away ten weeks; then I'll be back, with lots of cool stories to tell about NASA and things I heard and did. We've got

Google Talk to chat anytime. I'll text you guys everyday. I'll even write postcards. Totally 1960s."

"Do you get a Science credit for all that work?" Margot was the practical one.

"I forgot to ask. Doesn't really matter. I'm in this for the adventure."

"You always have adventures, Perry. We are jealous. Our lives are, like, boring movies where you can predict what will happen and how they will end," Rita said.

"Wherever I go, whatever I get myself into—you guys are there, understand? You are part of it. We are always going to be friends, okay? I love you guys."

Tears came, and noses were blown into tissues. Then the food came, and the gang was happily chatting again, gossiping about this and that. The Malt Shop. What a place!

The morning came. Perry was packed, and decided to carry the minimum, so his suitcase weighed less than 20 lb. He was too excited to eat more than a bowl of cereal with Gabby.

"Don't do anything crazy down there, Perry."

"Gabby! What do think I am? Just because I am out of the reach of my parents, and my older sister, doesn't mean I am going to lose control, and---like—hijack a space shuttle. Although that idea has some appeal, doesn't it?"

This was how things were between them. Teasing and affectionate wisecracks that revealed a deep bond between brother and sister. It was an anchor for Perry that he would need in years to come.

ACT II   BEYOND THE SKY

CHAPTER SIX   WHERE THE ANGELS DWELL

It had been three or four months now that Perry and Henry had been skywatching with others in the ASRAS club.

There was much more to just having access to equipment; these people took video and still images using the scopes. They gossiped endlessly about the hardware, the International Space Station live feed, what the Chinese lunar module *Chang-E* really saw, and so on.

And sometimes the topic of Unidentified Flying Objects would come up.

Online research showed that paranormal topics like UFOs were the second most popular Internet searches, right behind 'Sex'. With cell phone cameras and the heightened awareness of space and space travel in the media, more people in more countries were watching the skies than ever before. Everyone knew about the famous Roswell Crash of 1947, about Area 51, and its alleged secret space program, and much, much more.

Perry was still a neophyte to such discussions. He was just trying to be open, be logical, and stick to his principles as a junior scientist. *Seek a rational explanation, apply scientific knowledge, before you step out into wild speculation and emotionally biased perceptions.* This was the code that Perry lived by.

"You are too young to remember the Hudson Valley Sightings, but I saw them!" A young university postdoc was speaking to the Perry and Henry, one dark evening.

"Thousand of witnesses, dozens of sightings of mysterious boomerang crafts moving over the Hudson Valley, for what reason? No one knows. But irrefutable proof that we are not alone."

UFOs in New York State? The idea was intriguing. Perry was thinking about UFOs in space, maybe, or in another star system.

But of course, it makes sense that ETs might travel to Earth, to investigate us, or build a connection. He preferred to ignore the Hollywood version of a hostile alien force arriving from space. That could happen, too. But better to focus on the positive, Perry thought.

It was Perry's turn to speak.

"What about Planet X, or whatever? What evidence have you that it exists, and is already influencing our climate, or gravitational field?"

Several joined the discussion.

"There are papers suggesting, hypothetically, that such a body, if it exists, would cause certain perturbations in gravitational fields of the planets in our system," Peter, a grad student in Astrophysics, was saying.

"And the evidence is there. Something very large is on the edge of our solar system, but we are having trouble detecting it, for some reason. "

Peter spoke a little longer, but Perry was already thinking this might be his research focus for the summer, at JPL. They had telemetry, and access to world-class telescopes, both optical and infrared, and a new X-ray telescope. If something lurked out in space, he would find it, surely.

He realized what he would find at NASA would be far more complex a world than he had ever experienced. And, after all, he was still only eleven—going on twelve. He was going into 8th grade next fall. He was just a small player in a very big game involving government and research science. That was going to change a lot of things for Perry. And not necessarily for the better.

***

"I saw one," Henry said. "When we went camping with my cousins from Cleveland. It was over Lake Erie."

"Saw...a UFO, Henry? Really? How can you be sure?"

"Well I don't know for sure if it was an alien spacecraft, but it was an Unidentified, Flying, *Object*. It was like an orb of light. I was sure it was fireflies or something, but it shot over vast distances of the sky and turned, wobbled, and dived, like it was playing games, or something."

"Who else saw this?"

"We all did. My uncle says they have an underwater base in Lake Ontario, or Lake Erie, I forget which. He's seen them many times. He works late and sees them on his smoke breaks."

"That's freaky."

"We have to begin to allow Society to consider the fact that we are being visited, or maybe being infiltrated. Even people in the government are saying there has to be a Day of Disclosure about what the President and the Armed Forces know about all this."

"Wow, Henry. I didn't realize that this was a big thing for you."

"Perry, I just want science to explain what people are finding, witnessing. Something big is happening, Perry. I just know it."

"Yeah, I think you're right, Henry. Something big."

***

The flight to Los Angeles was a long one. They flew from Rochester, changed in Minneapolis, then on to L.A. Perry was too excited to eat or sleep the day before. His parents were typical adults, slightly tired and slightly grumpy.

But the sunshine was far brighter in California, just like all the songs say. Soon, they were in their hotel.

"We're only here this weekend, dear. Let's go get you some shirts and shoes that suit weather like this. Must be over 80° today. I can't breathe in this."

Perry took a selfie of him with his Mom—in sunglasses—and his Dad—wearing a Dodgers' ballcap. It was June.

It was the City of Angels, all four million of them. Spread out over 469 square miles of offices, malls, and suburbs in a teeming crowd of human busy-ness. Home of Hollywood, and everything modern and beautiful about America. There was the darker side, too, but all of it gave Los Angeles its unique and marvelous character.

NASA's Jet Propulsion Laboratory was managed by Caltech and was nestled in the hills east of the downtown core. Perry had to be screened, given an ID badge that doubled as an access key to his assigned lab. He was given a supervisor, but not a lab partner—at his own request. Perry wanted—preferred—to work alone.

Besides, he had a secret agenda that went far beyond his initial assignment.

The emphasis in JPL was robotics and space technology, so engineers were there in abundance. The summer interns, like himself, had quite a bit of freedom to choose a research subject. They also had unrestricted access to Mt. Wilson, which housed state-of-the-art telescopes that had given the United States its reputation as a world leader in astronomy. This is where Perry wanted to be.

"Sir? I want to do research into solar system features of interest such as the moons of the various planets, and what lies beyond Pluto and the dwarf planets."

"Very well, Perry. Do you know anything about telescopes?"

"A bit, sir. I have been working with my club at Rochester, and have my own small scope, and I am quite familiar with the names of the constellations and their position in the sky in all seasons."

"Good. That's the basics. I'm giving you special authorization to use the big scopes, day or night, with the understanding that you report what you see, in writing, each week. Are we in agreement on this?"

"Yes, sir."

'Sir' was his supervisor, who turned out to be Air Force Major Walsh out of Vandenberg AFB, who divided his time between JPL and the base. Which would turn out to be a very interesting thing, as the summer went on.

Most of what NASA was doing involved the military, sooner or later, which meant that there were levels of information that were not to be made public. These were called 'classified' files. Perry did not know that he would be pulled into matters of national security a lot faster than he could imagine.

Perry sent a text first to his parents, telling them he was okay, and then to Henry, updating him on what was going on down in Southern California.

"No way!" Henry said.

"It's true. I got special clearance with my supervisor, who is an Air Force officer."

"Oh man! Can you have visitors or guests? This is too amazing. What are you going to be watching for? Like I didn't already know! ☺"

"I plan to see what these mysterious satellites around Titan are up to, for starters. Then I want to see why the rings of Saturn itself have dark shadows that seem to be giant craft. And then...,"

Perry looked over his shoulder, and stepped out of range of the security camera. "Then, the thing that is out there just beyond our solar system, the thing they called Planet X. Does this make sense, Henry?"

"Totally. But what if you see something, or photograph something you are not supposed to see? Like a UFO, or something?"

"Well that's the thing, Henry. I am sure that I will. Do I tell the major? I am expected to. So then what happens? I always tell the truth, Henry, you know me."

"Geez, Perry. This could get really weird. Maybe they could swear you to secrecy, and you had to promise to never ever tell anyone. Even me. That sucks. But this is the Government, and they have to keep certain things secret, as everybody knows."

"I'll keep you posted, Henry. Should we ask Max and Margot how to set up a decoy email account that has a fake name and a fake profile? So we can chat, but it's not traceable back to either one of us? I don't know why I am even thinking this."

"You're scaring me, Perry. But sure, I will tell the gang. Gotta go. Later."

***

JPL was kind of like school in a way: everything was fitted into a strict timetable that everybody followed. They even had a cafeteria, way better than the one at Brackendale MS. They had sushi, and Tex-Mex, and submarine sandwiches made to order. They didn't have bells, of course, but people knew to the minute when lunch was over, or break was over.

At 5:00pm sharp, they powered off their computers in the Main Complex, put on their jackets, and raced to the parking lot. They called it the Five O'Clock Track Club.

But the nerds who were waist-deep in their experiments stayed on. Stayed very late, many days. They ordered in when they got hungry. Local restaurants were happy for the business, and delivered on time, every time. Pizza was the favorite.

So it was, that late one evening in early July, Perry overheard something that would motivate him to spend a lot more time at the observatory.

"Are you sure?" A hushed voice of a girl was speaking.

"Pretty sure. I checked it twice."

"Should we tell someone?"

"No, you idiot! We'll be in deep shit if we say a word about this!" The young man stood up and Perry could see him over the divider that sectioned off the monitoring area.

Perry had seen him before. Quite a lot, actually. He had a beard and glasses, and was probably one of the junior scientists who was hired after graduation from Caltech, or MIT, or Stanford. They only hired the best.

Then Perry realized that they had access to information that was, or should be, classified. Maybe this was one of those moments when scientists stumble upon something incredible, and then wonder what to do with it. Maybe Perry would get a sense of how to handle it from their conversation.

Should I let them know I am here? Will they take me into their confidence? Or maybe, like a spy movie, I will have to be killed and disposed of, because they know I am a witness?

Perry decided to stay still and crouch behind his cubicle wall. If he didn't make any noise, he could go on listening.

"Somebody has to know. If this is what we've been told to track, then why not just file a report?" The girl was trying to be calm, but her voice caught and was cut off.

"Ted, this is big. We could be fired, or worse, if we *don't* report it, and interrogated by the Air Force Office of Special Investigations if we *do*. This is trouble any way you look at it."

"We're not spies, or terrorists. We're scientists, for heaven's sake. We've got nothing to hide. We did nothing wrong."

"You're right. We did nothing wrong. We could have been mistaken, anyway. Data is not perfect, and neither are data scientists."

"So let's keep this thing under our hats, Macy, at least until we get more proof."

Then the conversation petered out. Soon after, the pair left the lab. It was seven o'clock. Perry was alone in the most sophisticated research site in the Western United States, or maybe the whole world!

He realized that closed circuit surveillance cameras were never sleeping, so he sauntered over to the console where the two had been working, and sat down like he belonged there. Like it was his workstation. The guards didn't know and probably didn't care. Just act cool and do what you gotta do.

Perry wanted to see what they saw.

The screen had lots of data and code. Could he make sense of any of it? Perry decided to look for anything quantitative that could reveal what part of space this data was related to.

There were only two lines of English, beneath some coordinates for something they were tracking.

Anomalous inbound object found and verified. Estimated time of solar system entry is 90-120 days.

The numbers were in Astronomical Units— one AU is the distance from the Sun to Earth. The data showed this thing to be 37AU distant from the point of observation—California, USA.

That meant it was exactly where Perry expected to find whatever was disturbing the gravitational fields on our planets, and maybe was responsible for increased earthquake activity in the Pacific and in East Asia. There were many people studying seismic increases and wondering why, all of a sudden, Planet Earth was becoming more unstable with every passing month.

He had to get to Mt. Wilson and see for himself.

CHAPTER SEVEN   WHAT THE INTERN SAW

Mt. Wilson has been a world-class astronomical observatory since 1906. It is best known for its two large telescopes: the 100-inch Hooker telescope, and a slightly smaller 60-inch telescope, that were dozens of times more powerful than anything Perry had worked with before. Being in the San Gabriel Mountains, Mt. Wilson did not have the smog and pollution of the city below, meaning stargazing was excellent from this altitude of 5700 ft.

Perry fiddled with the slip of paper in his wallet; the entry code. He also had to place his thumb on a keypad. Once this was done, the door lock popped and Perry was in to the viewing chamber. A ladder and scaffolding were placed by each scope, so Perry grabbed the handrail and climbed the stairs, up, up, till he reached the viewing platform itself. He was a good 40 feet above the concrete floor below, equivalent to a four-storey building.

These were reflectors, like the one he took from the Science room, so worked along similar lines: look in the eyepiece, adjust the apparatus to match the target using the targeting scope mounted on the side. The motor hummed as the enormous tube moved into position. The dome above was already open, as if waiting for Perry's command.

Perry could see what few humans had ever seen: Space, the vast regions beyond Earth and the Moon, beyond the planets and asteroids, out into the Milky Way galaxy, and then beyond that—into interstellar space.

It was easy to lose track of time here. There was so much to see! Only when his rumbling stomach and sore backside reminded him that he was human, not a machine, did he give some thought to coming down and going home.

'Home' was the student dorm at Caltech, off Hwy. 210 in Pasadena, and about a twenty minute cab ride from Mt. Wilson itself. Very convenient and safe for a young student from out of town.

He shared a room with a boy from Vancouver B.C., also a summer intern, also an astronomy geek. His family had immigrated to Canada from China, and he was a third year student at the well-known University of British Columbia in Vancouver. What was even weirder, his English name was Perry--Perry Rong Zhou.

The two Perrys got along just fine and often ate together in the cafeteria, or in a local café. They both were interested in astronomy and both dreamed of a career in science.

"Why did you apply for this program," Perry Normal asked.

"Same as you. I like space. I dream of space travel," Perry Zhou said.

"But you are further along than me. I'm only in seventh grade."

"That's cool. You'll be in university soon just like me. I want to work with cutting edge technology and see where this space program is going. If I write a paper I will get two credits for my undergraduate degree. Good, eh?"

"Awesome! Do all Canadians say 'eh' after they talk?"

Perry Zhou laughed. "Not really. I picked it up at school."

***

They did not work in the same lab area, and they had different goals. One was interested in engineering, and one was interested in some secret that was happening in space, and no one was supposed to talk about.

And that was the problem. Perry was witnessing two extraordinary events happening now in our own solar system. And he wanted to tell someone, he wanted to put it in his report to Major Walsh. But now he was scared. Scared to tell the truth.

He packed a lunch to bring to Mount Wilson because he planned to be there very late tonight. He was determined to gather more evidence that Earth may be in danger. Surely others have seen it, this massive thing hurtling in from deep space, from darkness, threatening our very existence.

It was cool and unearthly quiet inside the great hall where the telescopes were waiting, waiting for someone like Perry, to use them, to find the secrets of Space, and lead Humanity forward to a new age as Cosmic Citizens.

The larger of the two telescopes made a real difference in the detail and clarity of what Perry could see. He could see the cloudy veil of Titan, he could see the marvelous rings of that mighty giant, Saturn, its enormous bulk girdled with bands of blue and grey tones. You could fit 764 Earths into its massive size.

He could also see what seemed to be craft of some kind, moving in and out of the rings themselves, and orbiting Titan and passing under the clouds toward the surface, for purposes unknown.

***

"I have to tell somebody, Perry. I have to tell you. What I saw. What I think is happening."

Perry from Canada was dangling a piece of pepperoni pizza in front of his face, trying to get the tip of the slice to go into his hungry mouth.

"So, tell!"

"There's someone out there, on Titan. There's UFOs or something that travel back and forth to the main planet, Saturn. I don't know what they are doing but I keep seeing them; they're like bees going in and out of a hive. They flash and I need some ideas about why." Perry Normal was running out of breath he was speaking so fast.

"Ah, this is where I get off the bus, my young friend. All talk of UFOs and aliens and such are definitely not on my agenda."

"Besides, I'm Chinese Even though I'm actually a Canadian citizen, these paranoid government types will probably think I'm a spy and want to steal technology for the Chinese. Which couldn't be farther from the truth. But people are prejudiced."

"You're a white guy so you probably never felt suspicious eyes on you just because you are different, have a different ethnic background. But I feel it. I'm not ashamed of who I am and where I come from. I'm just a guy with dreams of getting a decent education and a decent career in a field I love. I can't be going off in some fringe of scientific inquiry that people will use against me. Besides, my parents are conservative. They want me to go into aeronautical engineering."

"So... sorry, Perry. You gotta go your own way, and I gotta go mine. Good luck, and don't say anything about what you may or may not have seen, to *anybody*. The real spies are in the military here. I'm off to meet my supervisor. Catch you later."

Perry couldn't move. He was pulled into the couch by the weight of what was just said. As always, Perry was alone with his thoughts, and his worries. No need to bother his parents, and he felt too bummed out to even text Henry.

Why did decisions about doing the right thing always seem to be complicated by what others want? Sometimes Perry Normal just wanted to be an eleven-year-old kid, and nothing else.

***

The photographs proved it. Right there, in the Cassini Mission folder, were crystal clear images of the things Perry had been watching. Images taken by NASA and therefore real, not fake, or Photo-shopped, or hoaxed by some hacker and posted online. These were proof that something was working on the rings, and maybe had a secret base on Titan or other moons. Was that why NASA and the European Space Agency was spending so much time looking at the moons of Saturn?

"They are right here, Henry! In full color! In fantastic detail! Why is nobody talking about this?" The boys, best friends, were texting like crazy.

"Maybe there is a logical explanation for it, Perry. We can't just jump to conclusions. If the space agencies thought it was important, I'm sure they would publish their findings in the news, or in the scientific magazines."

"Sure, okay, you're right, Henry. Maybe I'm freaking because these images are pretty much what I have been seeing, and they are so unexpected."

"What does your supervisor say about it?" Henry said.

"We haven't talked, really. He's a busy man at the air force base and I don't have any conclusions to give him. I don't want to bore him or take up his valuable time."

Perry was getting concerned now.

He hadn't heard from Major Walsh since he started.

"I'm just an intern, Henry. Nothing I say or think really matters. There are highly qualified people managing the space observations who know..." Perry's voice trailed off.

"Wait a second, Henry! I overheard a conversation a week ago." Perry told Henry the whole story of the two interns scanning space data, and what they said.

"Gee, Perry. That is kind of scary. What if there is something that will have a serious and maybe catastrophic effect on us here on Earth?"

"I know, Henry. That's what worries me even more than the presence of extraterrestrials in the vicinity of Saturn. So long as they stay out there and don't bother us down here on Earth, I don't have a problem with them."

"I sure wish I could come down and visit." Henry was wistful.

"Why don't you ask your parents? That would be amazing!"

"Naw, they want me to go to Summer School and get ahead in Science. I wonder what the hurry is? I'm going to be twelve in March. I won't need Physics for five more years. Anyway, that's the situation, Perry."

"Okay, Henry, I understand. I'll keep you updated, my friend. Good luck with Physics."

"Later."

Perry was disappointed, but he still had work to do himself.

Where are the pictures of deep space where this Planet X is found?

Perry found them, and a whole lot more.

CHAPTER EIGHT   SILENCE IS GOLDEN

"Sit down, Perry. You want a soda?"

"No, thank you, sir." Perry was tired after the drive from Pasadena to Vandenberg AFB, which was northwest of Los Angeles, near Santa Barbara on the Pacific Ocean.

Vandenberg was the site of Department of Defense satellite and missile launch facility and was home to several important space squadrons. It was one of the most important military installations in the United States. That's why Major Walsh spent 99% of his time here, rather than at JPL.

"So," the Major began. "You have questions for me?"

"Yes, sir. I actually do. It's about the objects—I don't really know what to call them— that I see through the telescopes at Mt. Wilson, and the corresponding images in the NASA files that you said I could look at, if I wanted."

"Uh-huh." A junior officer brought in a coffee and some snacks and placed them on the major's desk. "Something disturbed you. Am I right?"

"Well, Major Walsh, you see I am interested in the anomalies—the things that don't belong where they are, things that don't fit with our current thinking about Space."

Major Walsh took a long sip of coffee, and said: "Go on."

"Sir? I'm just a 7th Grader in a small American town. I am not good at lying, and I truly believe Science has the answers to all our questions. So just listen to what I have to say. This is the truth."

Perry explained about the flashes of light he saw and photographed at the observatory in Rochester. He told him that he saw it again from Mt. Wilson and their giant telescopes that show so much of the depths of our solar system in stunning detail. Then he said that his investigation of the Cassini and other NASA mission photographs, including some taken from the legendary Hubble Space Telescope, indicated that something was happening—out *there*.

"Who have you talked to about this?"

"No one really, sir. I have just made some notes in my journal and added my own photos to it."

"Good. Let's keep it that way. There's a couple of things I didn't mention, so now is a good time to talk about them."

Major Walsh talked a bit like Mr. Adams, the principal at Brackendale M.S. He talked like adults do when they want to discuss something important that may not turn out well for the kid they are speaking to. Like when you are in trouble. His voice had that tone, and Perry shifted uncomfortably in his chair.

"I think you know, Perry, that the information that you now have is secret; by that I mean it is not to be released to the media or the public. You cannot speak of it.

It's the same for all of us in the Air Force, and in the American military in general. We all sign an 'Oath of Secrecy' to ensure this rule is strictly followed. Following me?"

"Yes, sir."

"Our national security is our top priority. We know about certain things, like these unusual 'phenomena' that you saw, are of concern to us, and they *do* exist."

"But…" Major Walsh leaned closer over his desk and looked right at Perry.

"We must not disclose—tell—what we know or there could be panic or mass hysteria as soon as the television networks found out what we know, and did not tell. They don't understand or even seem to care that these secrets must remain secret. If the President wants people to know, he will tell them. We…keep our mouths shut. Simple as that."

"So, just to be clear, sir. Ah, UFOs exist, aliens exist, we know about them, they probably know about us. Is that what you are saying?"

"Precisely."

"Oh my gawd," Perry blurted out. "What about Planet X, sir? NASA and the American Association for the Advancement of Science have confirmed it. Is it going to hit us?"

"Well, don't get ahead of yourself, Perry. Yes, there is something huge at the edge of our solar system, but we don't know enough about it yet to say whether it is a threat to Earth or not. Not yet, not for certain.

You are a scientist, albeit a young one. Why not let Science continue its investigation, and you just follow along? Exciting discoveries will be released, and you can see it on National Geographic or Discovery Channel. Sound good?"

The major's voice now sounded like the conversation was over.

On the drive back to L.A., Perry's mind was whirling.

They know! They absolutely know! That answered a lot of questions people on the Internet were talking about. Conspiracy theory and coverups.

When Perry got back to his dorm at Caltech, the front desk informed him that he had been moved to another room.

His workstation at JPL had been moved, too. There was an official, sitting at a desk, that had a direct view of Perry's workspace. And a closed circuit TV camera was pointed right at him.

***

"Speech is silver, silence is golden." That's what his grandparents used to say. That's what Mrs. Busby said in English class when the kids got too noisy.

But that statement had new and sinister meaning for Perry.

He wanted to kick himself for being so honest with Major Walsh. He had said too much. He always jumped in and told people the truth. Now he was being watched.

No, stop it Perry, he told himself. *You did nothing wrong, at least not on purpose. Besides, he told you what the reality is: the Government knows about some spooky secret stuff going on in space, and they are studying it. End of story.*

Perry also realized that his own secret—to find out about those flashes and what they might mean—was what motivated him to come here in the first place. And now he had a piece of the answer. But could never tell anyone. *This is so frustrating*, thought Perry. *Science can't operate under a cloak of secrecy. It just can't.*

***

All the rest of that week, and into his final week in California, Perry continued to watch and wait, look and see what the night sky concealed.

Of course, there were many other wonders to behold: distant stars and galaxies light-years away, hovered in view. *Is someone watching us, too?* Perry mused.

It makes sense he decided. We humans are curious, and look outward into the Universe. We map the stars and constellations, we document every little thing that we discover. We have SETI in the desert: a whole array of satellite dishes that listens for signals that may have come from other civilizations, all the way to Earth.

The really interesting ones would be answers to the signals we already sent out years ago, and keep sending. Humans want to connect with our space neighbors; that much was clear.

The information that Perry was getting had an incredible meaning: it was actually happening! Now!

And Perry Normal, Junior Scientist, was a witness—no, a *participant*, in a coming event when this would be revealed, what Internet surfers called 'The Day of Disclosure'. A spaceship might land on The White House lawn. The President would be smiling, and human history would change forever.

And the TV cameras would be interviewing Perry, and congratulating him on his contribution.

Yeah, right!

Perry stood up and stretched. Everyone in the lab was gone by five, as usual. He left his journal and all that it contained on his desk, intending to clean it up the next morning.

But the next morning it was gone—all of it!

"Excuse me, sir." Perry was speaking to the official sitting at the desk.

"Did someone come in this morning, and maybe go to my work area? That you saw?"

"I saw no one in your area. Anything else?" His tone was sharp, even rude.

"No, thank you, sir." *Thanks for nothing, idiot!* Perry was pissed off. *You sit there all day doing nothing but didn't see who stole my file! Loser!*

Now what? Perry wondered. His guidebook with the entry codes to JPL and Mt. Wilson was also missing.

All they left him was a computer screen and a pencil. Not even any scraps of paper. He had to dig some out of the recycling bin.

Tomorrow, the taxi would drive him to LAX, and he would catch a flight to Rochester, where his parents would pick him up, and welcome him back to his familiar world in Brackendale, New York.

Well, at least his friends would be sitting at The Malt Shop and he could tell them—what?? Who knows? Perry would decide what to share, what he felt it was *right* to share.

But the military wasn't quite finished with Perry Normal yet.

***

"Sit down, Mr. Normal." There were armed guards at attention at the door of a windowless room that was in the basement of the JPL complex.

It wasn't normal for Perry to be called by his family name. It usually meant you were in serious trouble. Like right now.

"Is this your file?" A military officer in uniform was sitting behind a desk, while Perry faced him from a bench and table, about ten feet in front.

"Yes, sir."

"This file now belongs to the government. Do you understand?"

"Not really. What did I do?" Perry was raising his voice but since his voice was starting to break as it does for boys at that age, it came out like a squeak from a frightened squirrel.

"Are you a spy? Who are you working for?"

"Brackendale Middle School, Science Department. Sir."

"Maybe you are one of those media activists that stir up conspiracies, although you look a little bit young. Have you been taking photographs?"

"They were all in my journal, which has somehow disappeared, sir. Only pictures of unusual objects that caught my attention. Or planets and stars. I got one of a meteor streaking in the area of Constellation Cygnus, but I wasn't sure that..."

The interrogator cut him off.

"What do you know about aliens?"

"You mean 'illegal immigrants'? Not much. We don't get many in Brackendale."

"Quit stalling, young man. I know you know something. Spit it out."

"Only what Major Walsh told me. That someone is establishing a presence in the region of Saturn and its moons, and the government is looking into it, and that I should look elsewhere for amusement when I use the telescope."

"What if I told you *I* was an alien?" The officer suddenly looked a shade more scary, and his eyes darker than ink, and his ears suddenly seemed more pointed.

"You don't have an accent, sir."

"You are the perfect plant. No one would suspect a kid. An American kid. Maybe that's how Edward Snowden started out. A kid with unnatural curiosity."

"Who is Edward..."

The military officer stood up, and summoned the guards.

"Take this boy back to JPL, and tell admin to book him a flight. I want him out of here by tomorrow."

"Sir!" The hand lifted in a salute.

A uniformed Marine gripped Perry firmly by his upper arm and hustled him toward a waiting jeep. The tarmac was so hot it made wavy heat mirages, that made the whole experience seem completely surreal.

Soon Perry was passing through Santa Barbara, that beautiful town on the edge of the great Pacific. But Perry did not get to do any sightseeing today.

The driver gave him a cold soda and a bag of chips, which was nice, because Perry was getting hungry, especially now that the dread of being stood up in front of a firing squad was wearing off.

Perry felt like he should feel guilty, or something, but he had done nothing illegal, nothing like what real spies do: hack computers, photograph classified documents, break into secure facilities with intent to steal secrets. Why did he feel guilty? Or maybe he was just ashamed that his summer internship had come to a crashing conclusion.

Maybe there really *was* a spy or terrorist on the loose in the NASA network that was spread across twelve states and ten cities, but it wasn't Perry. He wanted them to acknowledge that. Hopefully, they would send a letter to his parents admitting he was never a security threat or nuisance during his sojourn in Los Angeles. If Perry was lucky.

Chapter Nine   With A Shadow of Doubt

It was mid-August when the first letter arrived.

It had an official NASA logo on the envelope and the paper inside. Perry was thinking this is to say 'thanks' for your work in supporting the United States Space Program as a volunteer. But the letter was quite different.

His mother sat down on the couch to read it. She *never* sat down, unless something serious had come up.

"Robert? You should read this. It's about Perry."

Robert Normal was a financial analyst and he was as down to earth as anybody could get.

"Perry? Was there some trouble while you were there?" His Dad looked troubled.

"Ah, well Dad, I was just doing what they told me I *could* do. I didn't touch anything I wasn't supposed to, and I didn't talk to anybody outside of NASA about what I was doing."

"Well then I can't understand why they say these things about you. 'Put national security at risk', 'failed to comply with regulations'. What did you do?"

Perry's stomach was in knots. His mouth was dry. This is what he expected it would be like when they caught him stealing the Science telescope, which didn't happen, of course. Perry's luck now seemed to have run out.

"I saw some things, Dad. In the telescope. Some things that nobody seems to have talked about at NASA. My supervisor, Major Walsh, told me to never mention any of it, so I agreed, and I thought he was cool with it."

"Go on."

"Then they interrogated me for three hours at Vandenberg, which was a big shock. I thought the Major had worked things out with me. We had an agreement. Then my files at my desk totally disappeared, and someone changed my dorm room and took the time to search through all my stuff, for some reason."

"I thought they were looking for drugs or a gun, like I was an enemy planted there to cause an interruption in their operations. I felt like I was in a movie and, like, The Terminator was going to come out of the bathroom and stuff me in a sack and take me who-knows-where."

"The can't do that, can they, Robert?" His Mom was getting upset now.

"I don't know, Lisa. He was on a military base and the rules are different. Doesn't matter if you are a civilian or serviceman—if they want to question you, they can."

"But he's a kid, in 7th grade, not an ISIS agent, or something. They invited him. And we paid for him to go. Not to be treated like a criminal. I'm going to contact our Congressman. This is a violation of our son's civil rights."

But it was the next two letters that really set Lisa Normal off.

They were addressed to the school principal, and to Mr. Matson, the Head of the Science Department. They didn't state that Perry had compromised national security, or accessed classified information. It was far worse than that.

***

"Mr. and Mrs. Normal, we are as disturbed about this as you are," Principal Adams began.

"What their allegations suggest is not what we have come to believe about Perry. But we must take it seriously, all the same."

"What are you talking about, Mr. Adams?"

Lisa Normal worked for the school board administration and was known to be a firm and responsible woman in the organization.

She had her game face on now. Her son was on trial and she was going to defend him.

"What they are saying...ah, suggesting, no, implying, is that Perry is, ah, mentally unstable. That the things he claimed to have experienced are pure fantasy, like the hallucinations of a madman, and that he should receive psychiatric help as soon as possible."

"Whaat?!" Mrs. Normal's voice rose to a shriek.

Perry was not present at the meeting, so he was told later by some students that she could be heard all the way down the main hall of the school.

"We have a school psychologist, as you must know, as a board administrator. We strongly suggest that Perry get tested, or assessed, or whatever it is that they do.

We know this must be a bit of a shock for you…"

Mrs. Normal cut him off.

"A shock? This is outrageous! Do you hear me, Mr. Adams?

I will *not* subject my son to a psychiatric evaluation based on a letter from a military officer, who is probably a nutcase himself.

No! I tell you what we are going to do.

We are going to shred this letter, and any copies you made, and then forget this whole damned situation even came up.

Perry will continue his classes in 8th grade, along with his peers, and have a fulfilling and meaningful year of academic studies at Brackendale.

Do I make myself clear, Mr. Adams?"

If Mr. Adams could have crawled under his desk, he would have.

Mr. Matson was red-faced, but a tiny smile appeared at the corner of his mouth.

Mr. Normal stood up to announce this meeting was over. He shook Mr. Adams' hand, as if to say: 'Better do what she says'.

The door to the principal's office flew open, and two parents on fire left the General Office like pterodactyls after a kill.

And that was the end of the matter.

***

Perry started school, along with two hundred and sixty-five other middle school children, rested after summer vacation, and ready to get down to business. The familiar teachers were in their classrooms, the cafeteria food was as boring and tasteless as always, and the lockers were assigned in an orderly fashion that no computer could possibly have done. It was September.

"This fall we are going to learn to read and analyze the essay form of Literature," said Mrs.

Busby in her usual cheerful voice. She seemed to like teaching middle school children things that the students often wondered would be relevant in a digital world.

"Don't they have an app for this?" muttered Robert.

"This isn't the 19th Century anymore," said Margot.

Margot was the school superstar in everything computer. Hardware, software, shareware, malware; Margot knew everything there was to know, and even the teachers and school secretary quietly consulted with her about the annoying little problems that came up constantly.

There was no computer department or tech on hand to do these things. Even the school board had a technician who was difficult to find when someone needed him. Someone hinted that he smoked weed and then lost track of time, or forgot what he was supposed to be fixing at the moment. Whatever.

"But what is really really exciting, boys and girls," Mrs. Busby was almost singing the words,

"...is that in the winter term we are going to learn how to write essays ourselves, properly, using a carefully constructed thesis. Isn't that exciting?"

Randy the Gorilla, who always found a seat at the back of every class, could be heard to say— none too quietly—"Yeah, about as exciting as a fart in a spacesuit."

"So open your books, boys and girls, and let's begin with one of America's favorite authors who was a master essayist: Ralph Waldo Emerson."

Randy and Mike were falling over laughing.

"Waldo. Waldo. What kind of name is that? Hardy-har-har."

"He has much wisdom to offer those who care to listen," said Mrs. Busby huffily.

"Now," she instructed. "Open your books to Page 86 and begin reading 'Self-Reliance'." There were groans and sighs, but everyone did as they were instructed. She was much better that Mr. Krushchevsky, the Math teacher.

Mr. Krushchevsky spoke with a heavy Russian accent, as he had recently come from Moscow.

"Now cluss. I vill tell you za difference between Russian students and American students. Pay attention." The Crusher rolled his 'r's in a dramatic way, so 'Russian' scunded like 'Hrrrrussian'.

Mr. Krushchevsky was not that tall, but very large in a certain way.

Perhaps it was his shoulders, that spoke of his wrestling days in the Russian military, or his growing gut that now required him to wear suspenders instead of a belt, in order to keep his trousers up.

He was large, and if he were a teddy bear, and might be kind of cuddly. Not really like the Russian bear, the national symbol of that huge country.

"In Russia, we *train* students. We don't let them grow like weeds, or run wild like foxes. We train you body and mind. We begin Mathematics in first grade to teach basic number theory. By Seventh Grade, we know more Math than you have learned by your senior year. This fundamental knowledge leads to future success in engineering, and in industry."

Randy the Gorilla then said the unspeakable, as he usually did, just blurting out the question.

"Then why did you come to America, if Russia is so great?"

Mr. Krushchevsky turned red—but not purple. If he turns purple, you are in deep trouble.

"So that America can benefit from Russia's academic excellence. I immigrated to this country because I love the freedom, and opportunities to use what I know. Teaching you undisciplined Yankees is my fate, I'm afraid."

He turned to the chalkboard and began to scribble a basic theorem in Geometry, sketching a triangle to demonstrate. Nevertheless, a Russian word nobody knew of course, escaped his lips.

Henry wrote it down. Or what it sounded like to them.

Durack. Google Translate said it meant 'idiot, fool' in Russian slang.

This was a reference to the class as a whole, and Randy in particular.

Henry passed this around on a note and the whole class started giggling.

"Vot is funny? Write zis. Write zis famous theorem from Pythagorus. Is foundation of all geometric forms."

Mrs. Latimer, the Socials teacher from Canada, was also an immigrant, if you thought about it. She married an American professor at SUNY, and they were expecting a baby sometime next year. Girls in the class were endlessly discussing her swelling belly, and the new wardrobe she would need to accommodate it, and what a good baby name would be. Boys never even noticed.

"Let's look at the movement started by Tom Paine, to motivate the patriots to begin the Revolution that would see America break away from the authority of King George and British control over the Thirteen Colonies."

And so it went. Days turned into weeks, and weeks turned into... assignments. There was an air of constant rushing to and fro as students divided up in groups, shared the tasks, trooped into the library to get help from Miss Floon, and line up at the printer to print out their final product to hand in.

Miss Floon reminded them of her upcoming seminar in citing references and writing a bibliography. She said it like it was expected that every student in Brackendale should attend, or their hair would fall out, or something.

There were quizzes and the dreaded midterm tests just ahead. Perry Normal, the science whiz, was being texted and emailed like a rock star.

It was widely believed that he could solve any problem, or devise a creative idea for a project effortlessly, ideas that resulted in A or A+ grades for the fortunate student who submitted them. Perry dismissed such rumors.

Besides, Perry had his own work to do. Just like everyone else. Except that this NASA business was not quite over. Not by a long shot.

CHAPTER TEN   MEN IN BLACK

"Who are those guys?" said Rita.

"Yeah, and look at the weird car they are driving. A total antique," Max said.

Max loved cars, as many boys do, and he identified this particular mysterious vehicle as a 1957 Cadillac DeVille, in mint condition, with fins that would make any shark proud to be seen with.

The vintage pink Caddy was just parked across the street from the school. They seemed to be waiting for someone.

The bell rang and the throng of students rushed the doors, throwing them open, and bursting like a wave of pure noise on the typically quiet neighborhood.

The two men wearing odd, wraparound sunglasses, watched one boy in particular, and when Perry got on his bike and pedaled down Newton Ave., they started the big car, pulled a u-ee, and sped after him.

Robert texted Perry on his cell.

"Hey! Perry! Watch out for the two weirdoes in an old pink car, who are tailing you. Dunno who they are, but I get bad vibes from them. Take the secret back alley route we used to go home by. Once you get there, lock the door, and text me."

Perry felt the buzz of his phone and dug it out of his pocket. He read Robert's message. Just in time, too.

The powerful Cadillac was approaching fast.

Perry swung the handlebars sharply to the right at the alley and made a series of swift maneuvers, cut across the park, and disappeared in the alley behind his house.

He had eluded them, for now.

Once safely in his room, he texted Robert, and Henry. Henry knew about the legendary Men in Black, and Perry was now convinced they were more than just an urban legend: they were real.

And they were after him, for some unknown reason.

'Henry! When you get this, call me right away.'

Five minutes later, Henry called.

"Hey, Perry. What's up?"

"Henry. Robert said an old pink car with two Men in Black was following me after school. Did you see them?"

"No way! Too bad! I was in the Science Lab finishing my experiment. How did you escape?"

"The secret route. They couldn't get that big pig into the narrow alley, and I was gone before they could circle onto Edison Street.

What do they want, Henry? We have to talk. Can you come over, and scope out my street on the way? If you see anything, hide or take a photo with your cell."

Henry arrived, disappointed that he had failed to detect the pink car and its strange occupants. Henry knew about MIBs, however.

"They often show up after somebody has a so-called 'close-encounter', some kind of UFO contact or sighting."

"Why? Are they government agents trying to hush up a witness to the event so many people have reported? Even the media are reporting UFO sightings and stuff, now."

"They probably are. But there are still some who think they are actual aliens who have reasons of their own for keeping witnesses quiet."

Perry crossed his arms.

"This is too freaky, Henry. Whoever they really are, I do not want to meet them, talk to them, go with them—anywhere."

"Hey, maybe they can trade some technology that makes school easier, like software that does your homework for you—any subject! Upload it, then it uses your printer to scan the assignment, and prints out an amazing and original piece of work, spellchecked, and referenced, so even Miss Floon would gasp at it. Wouldn't that be cool?"

Perry looked at Henry.

"What do I trade with an advanced civilization that has come to Earth for unknown purposes, and chases schoolkids down the street?"

Henry held up his finger.

"Your bicycle, Perry. It is such primitive technology that they could spend years studying its mechanism."

"Oh, please, Henry," said Perry, rolling his eyes.

Then Perry had another thought.

"Wait, Henry. What if I traded a Maxi-burger, fully loaded, with fries and a chocolate shake, one for each of them? They can't get that anywhere! Not on their planet. And not on this planet, unless they go to The Malt Shop."

They both laughed at their silly jokes.

Outside the front window, a large pink car was passing, slowly, like a falcon seeking prey, never stopping until it finds what it is looking for.

"You gotta go, Henry. It's nearly dinnertime. Your folks will be waiting, and mine will be home soon. If you're lucky, maybe your Mom got Chinese takeout from Emperor's Garden. Text me!"

***

The next day the car was not waiting across the street for Perry. It had gone.

Maybe they had the wrong kid.

Or maybe they had the wrong Brackendale.

Aliens can get GPS coordinates wrong, too, Perry reassured himself.

Maybe they got the wrong planet. It's a big universe!

As things turned out, this time it was Henry's turn to be stalked, by men in black suits, with larger than normal heads, and eyes that seemed almond-shaped underneath their RayBans.

They were kind of skinny and walked stiffly, like when your legs fall asleep and they are all pins and needles, and don't work properly for a few minutes.

Henry watched in fascination as the pink car parked in front of their garage, beside the hedge. The men came up the front walk and rang the doorbell. Mrs. Schuyler answered.

"Yes? Can I help you?"

"We want to see your son."

No 'please', no friendly facial expression. So rude!

"Henry? Somebody is here, dear."

Henry came up behind his Mom and poked his head out the door.

That's when he realized that they were apparently not human! He yelled instinctively and pulled back into the house.

"Your boy is not Normal."

They both spoke simultaneously, in a robot monotone.

"No, he is Henry Gerrit Schuyler. And who are *you*?"

"We want to have Normal."

Mrs. Schuyler was losing patience.

"Then act like it! And take off those ridiculous sunglasses. It's October."

The Men in Black took a step back, like they were joined together at the hip.

"And tell your mother to buy you a suit that fits you."

The robot voices spoke in unison.

"Can we park in your driveway?"

"Looks like you already did."

"We are hungry."

Suddenly, Mr. Schuyler returned from his walk with Duke, the family Doberman, who began barking furiously, and snapped viciously at the Men in Black.

They turned to look at the dog and asked: "Is this good to eat?"

Mrs. Schuyler reacted with fury.

"Stay away from our dog, stay away from our house, and stay away from our son!"

Mr. Schuyler reined in Duke on his leash, and spoke.

"Hey!! Men in Black! Cool Hallowe'en costumes! Super-realistic!" Then he took the dog through the gate to the backyard.

Henry decided there was something he absolutely *had* to do.

He stepped out onto the porch, inched closer, and took a selfie with the MIBs. This was proof and Henry knew it. This would be classic.

The flash seemed to blind the two men, who stumbled down the steps to the driveway, piled into their car, and backed out roughly onto Copernicus Crescent, scraping the muffler on the concrete apron.

The tires squealed as they accelerated and vanished into the dusk.

"You have to choose your friends more carefully, Henry. Those scientists are a bit too old for you to be hanging around with. Now, let's have supper."

ACT III   BEYOND BELIEF

CHAPTER EIGHT   WHAT GOES AROUND...

"That is incredible, Henry."

"I know. Look at their faces!" Henry was showing Perry the two selfies he snapped on his front porch.

"Yeah, their faces are, like, made of wax, or putty. But no, I meant, it is strange that they dialed in on your house when they were really trying to track *me* down.

How do they know that we are friends? That you live three streets over from me, and like skywatching for UFOs? Were they watching us all along?"

"Maybe," said Henry. "Or maybe they hacked our cell phone records and then looked up my name and address."

"It doesn't make sense. They said 'We want Normal', meaning me—Perry Normal. If they hacked us, why didn't they show up at *my* house, instead of yours?"

"Their Garmin GPS software is out of date?"

The boys were laughing, but there were clearly unanswered questions. Maybe it didn't matter now. The MIBs were gone, and had not returned.

Maybe Perry could finally relax and put this whole thing behind him.

***

It wasn't that Perry's close pals saw themselves as anything special. They just preferred to hang together since they shared classes and teachers, went through English and Math and Social Studies and Gym class together. They were all in the same boat, Robert's Dad liked to say. Robert's answer was 'Yeah, like a lifeboat of shipwreck survivors'.

So it was unusual that Big Mike, The Gorilla's best buddy, and resident tough guy at Brackendale, quietly approached Perry and Henry one day after Science class.

"Hey. Can I talk to you guys about something?"

"Sure, Mike. What's up?"

"Not here." He motioned with his finger and they left the school altogether, walking toward the park two blocks down Newton Blvd., turning right on Taddle Creek Drive.

Mike sat on a picnic table, and lit a smoke.

"You guys are, like, space-nuts, right? You study all this stuff about other planets and space travel?"

Perry sat on the bench near him, and Henry stood near Perry.

"Well, here's the thing. Something happened."

Perry shifted to face Mike squarely. "Ok, what?"

"I was meeting someone here last Sunday, late. I was waiting over there."

Mike pointed to an area near the trees. The park itself was quite large, and had natural forest and a creek that was different from the baseball diamond and bleachers area near the street.

"All of a sudden, a really bright light came down on me. I looked but could only see what looked like the edges of a metallic craft of some kind. It was turning or rotating, or whatever you call it.

I tried to run but I passed out. I hadn't been drinking or smoking weed, if that's what you are thinking."

"No, no, not at all," said Perry. "Go on."

"When I came to, I was in a room like a hospital or medical clinic. These fucking weird things with big black eyes were looking down on me, and I wanted to punch their little grey faces but I couldn't lift my arms or legs. Like I was paralyzed."

Henry butted Perry over and sat beside him on the bench. No one was in the park except a young mother with a stroller over near the swings, at least eighty yards away.

"I heard them talking but their lips weren't moving; then they stared right at me with those bug eyes.

That scared the shit out of me, Perry. It really did. I didn't know where I was, who they were, and what the fuck was going on!"

Mike pulled out his pack of smokes, and lit a new one from the glowing butt of the old one.

"You want one?"

"No, no thanks," Perry said. Henry shook his head.

"They took some blood in a needle, and poked me all over the place, like I was some piece of meat from Jerry's Market. Fuckers!

Anyways, I tried to look around and tell myself to remember all that, and then I woke up face down on the grass, wanting to puke.

I swear I'm not making this up! There's no way I was drinking on Sunday night. Got school the next day, right?"

"Yeah, right," Perry said.

"Can we walk over to where this happened?" Henry said.

"Gives me goosebumps, but sure, let me show you where this all went down."

The boys trooped over to a burned area that did not seem to have any trace of a campfire (which was not allowed in the park), but had a blackened ring, and all the grass and dandelions in the middle were fried, in that one spot.

"Here?" said Perry.

"Yes, this is the spot. This is where I always score my weed from a guy I know. I come here every other week, so I know my way around this park better than the old grannies who come to sit on a bench and chew their cud."

Perry knelt and touched the shriveled vegetation inside the ring. It crumbled like powder, indicating that intense heat had vaporized the water in the cells of each plant.

Did this prove Mike's bizarre story? Or was there a more ordinary explanation for the burn marks.

And where would Mike get the information about alien abductions so he *could* make up a story like this? Mike barely read his Grade 7 textbooks.

"This is interesting," was all that Perry could come up with at the moment.

"Look, Perry. I am so fucking freaked out I don't know who to talk to, so I picked you guys. Do you think this really happened, or have I totally lost it?!"

Perry gazed steadily at Mike.

"No, I don't think you have lost your mind, Mike. I think something happened to you, but I have no clear idea what. I get that you are kind of messed up about whatever it was."

Henry then dropped a bombshell.

"I saw the light, Perry.

I was in my bedroom with my binoculars last Sunday, looking at the Mars-Venus conjunction, and I saw a beam of light that appeared out of nowhere over the area of the park and the creek."

"Why didn't you tell me, Henry?"

"Forgot. I was so worried about The Crusher's geometry test this week that I forgot about it, until now."

Mike jumped off the table and rubbed his legs vigorously.

"See? Told you! I didn't make any of this up.

A fucking UFO zapped me, right here in this shitty little park in Brackendale, New York, and there was nothing I could do about it.

You think I'm gonna tell this story to the cops? Think again!"

Mike was walking in circles, smoking and repeating himself in strong language.

"Let's do this, Mike. Just try and be cool with it. Something bad happens doesn't mean it will happen again. But, just in case, stay out of the park, and spend lots of time at The Malt Shop, or The Eight-Ball, where people congregate. You'll be alright, man."

Perry never expected himself to be comforting a muscular guy nearly a foot taller who had a reputation as a moderately tough badass, but he slapped Mike on the shoulder pretty firmly, the way guys do to each other to say 'No worries'.

***

But Mike *was* worried. So was Perry, although he managed to hide it.

Was this something that had to do with the MIBs, or the military intimidation that he endured in the summer?

Or was it just a random chaotic event that happens to somebody who is in the wrong place at the wrong time?

Perry was sitting with Henry, musing about what a bizarre experience Mike seemed to have had.

"Henry, we need to keep our eyes open. And for gawd's sake—tell me if you see weird phenomena going on in our own neighborhood!

I've been so focused on outer space, that I forgot that our atmosphere is like a window that anybody *out there* can look into, or penetrate with their spacecraft.

We are like sitting ducks. That bothers me. A lot." Perry glanced up instinctively.

"Hey, why don't we report this 'incident'? Not to the police; we don't want to be laughed at. I mean, to a real UFO investigator, like someone from MUFON."

"That's actually not a bad idea, Henry. Why didn't *I* think of that?

They have the experience and knowledge about these things. Let's find them. They have people all over the country."

Chapter Nine   What Are We Looking For?

So it was that Perry made a vital connection in the complex world of space investigation. Turned out that one of the members of ASRAS was part of the local chapter of The Mutual UFO Network of America.

The Barkers picked them up, as they did before, for the ride to Rochester and the monthly get-together of the Astronomical Society of the Rochester Academy of Science at the Farash Center for Observational Astronomy in a suburban area. Perfect for dark-sky viewing. They had a meeting room inside that was comfortable and had audio-visual equipment that was far better than that at school.

Everyone greeted Perry and Henry warmly. Perry knew that they were not aware of his little sojourn in JPL in California, and considering how it turned out, he preferred to keep it that way. *'No muss—no fuss,'* as his Gramps liked to say.

The subject of the meeting was so shocking that Perry almost forgot why they came tonight.

Actually they wanted to find the MUFON representative. They didn't know if was a lady or a man. Henry joked that he hoped it wasn't an EBE-Extraterrestrial Biological Entity.

A man spoke into the microphone, which squealed briefly, until the volume was adjusted. There were perhaps fifty people in the audience, including some media reporters with national networks. Perry wondered why.

"It has come to our attention that a deep-space object the size of Jupiter—our largest planet, the gas giant that has a mass 318 times that of our Earth—is approaching our solar system at increasing velocity.

Folks. We have a problem!"

Tonight's guest speaker was an astronomer from a sister club in Syracuse.

He looked like a stereotypical nerdy scientist: glasses with black frames, a tie that was too skinny, pants that didn't reach down to his shoes, and a nervous habit of clearing his throat every ten seconds or so.

"Enh-engh. So I think we need to put our heads together and make a submission to

Washington that a strategy for dealing with this needs to be developed."

Cameras flashed, and reporters scribbled in their notebooks.

Perry and Henry struggled to peer over the heads of the people in the row in front of them.

Clearing his throat, the man continued.

"Now I know that NASA disputes all of this, and that the media go along with whatever NASA says, but we need to have another opinion, and that's why I am touring the country and speaking out."

After the talk, people gathered and debated over coffee and croissants. Perry wanted to find the MUFON rep.

"Excuse me? Are you Perry Normal?"

A tall, attractive twenty-something lady was standing in front of the boys in the foyer of the observatory.

"Yes, I am. Ah, to what do I owe this pleasure?"

Perry heard this one on TV and thought it would be a cool way to respond to a stranger.

"I am Macy Lawrence, and I work for—volunteer really—for the Mutual UFO Network. I was as Caltech this summer and I was working in the CNEOS SpaceScan project. I found out that you were there at the same time, as an intern, right?"

"That's right. Wait. You worked on the deep-space radar, and one night you and some guy saw something on the screen that frightened you guys a lot."

"How would you know *that*?" Macy's eyes grew wide.

"I overheard—I wasn't eavesdropping or anything like that, but I couldn't help hearing that you discovered something that had to be kept...ah, 'quiet'."

"Yes. That is true. I never dreamed anybody had heard us. Did you tell?"

"No. No! But I wanted so badly to share with you my own observations in the Mt. Wilson facility. About *it*. Planet X. Niburu. Wormwood. The Red Dragon."

Macy smiled a sexy smile. "I see you have been doing your homework, Perry."

"How did you know that I was there?" Perry said.

"There was an internal memo circulated, the day they cleaned your desk out, that this individual was not to be involved in any discussions or given any information 'until further notice'. It gave your name, and had a photo of you on it.

Like a 'WANTED' poster from the days of the outlaws of the Old West!"

Perry was not amused. "And so you saw me here tonight, and decided to tell me...what?"

"That what you were into, am I am a pretty good guesser, was top secret and classified, and you screwed up somehow, and they were erasing your presence at JPL."

"That is so unfair! Perry never did anything bad!" Now it was Henry.

"I totally believe you. Perry? I think we should talk. Somewhere more private."

***

"I was in the Near-Earth Tracking program at JPL until 2007, when it ceased operations due to funding cuts, or...I don't know. It has been rebooted under another name, and we work closely with the European Space Agency to track Near-Earth Objects.

We are using satellite technology that the Canadians have developed and put into space, and visual and other telescopes to monitor the area inside the Kuiper Belt, but outside the orbit of Pluto.

That is how we discovered Planet X. Percival Lowell, the great astronomer, believed it existed and was affecting our solar system. He was right.

Are you with me?"

Perry and Henry nodded at the same time. Macy was cute, and somehow her scientific knowledge was making her even more attractive, right at the moment.

"The Spaceguard Foundation wants this information out there. The U.S. Air Force and Space Command do not. The President has not been informed, and word on the street says he will not be told anything until the time is right."

"Does this have anything to do with aliens, and UFOs, miss?" Henry couldn't keep himself from blurting out what was on his mind.

"Well, Henry. That is where I put on my MUFON hat.

We investigate and record 'close encounters' of every kind, from every part of America—including Alaska and Hawaii. We have a liaison with similar organizations in Canada, the U.K., and Australia—which has a very active community of UFO observers and experiencers, by the way."

"That is kind of what I...we...wanted to share with you, but we didn't know you, or who, was the MUFON contact here."

"You're looking at her!" Again, that smile.

Perry was starting to notice girls more. They were not just the annoyances they seemed to be in 5th and 6th grade. They were fascinating, in their own right.

"We want to report an incident that happened to a friend of ours in Brackendale, quite recently."

Perry, with Henry's occasional interruptions, told her about Mike's alleged encounter in Nikola Tesla Park. He didn't leave out a single detail.

Macy made some notes on her phone. She got Perry's and Henry's emails, and said she would log this report this week.

"Wait! Before you go. What about this situation with Planet X? Do we continue to watch for it? I got a lot of flak from Air Force Intelligence for even mentioning that I saw it. They threatened me with jail if I mentioned it---publicly, at least. Can they put a twelve-year-old in jail, Macy?"

Her face took on a serious expression.

"You could be in danger so long as this is secret, so long as the government remains in denial about any Planet X or asteroid that may impact Earth. Let's just say that—for the time being—you do what Major Walsh told you to do.

"Wait a second. How do you know about Major Walsh?"

"Who do you think our supervisor was at JPL? Who do you think the girl was who left the screen on that night so someone like you could see what we were seeing?"

Perry stood like a tree hit by lightning. Flames could be shooting out his ears.

"Zip the lip! I'll be in touch."

Macy left for the parking lot, and two young science geeks were left standing in the full moonlight as it streamed through the twenty-foot windows of the Marian and Max Farash Center for Observational Astronomy.

CHAPTER TEN   THE DRAKE EQUATION

Perry asked Mr. Subramanian if he could do a Science project as a follow-up to his summer internship.

Since Perry's mother had spoken to Principal Adams about the matter in August, the doors to the Science Lab and everything in it were again opened to Perry.

So Perry just pretended that he had learned lots of cool things at JPL and wanted to build on them. And of course, get a Science credit with an excellent mark.

Mr. Subramanian taught the Astronomy unit in the curriculum, and he would be the staff mentor for any of these kinds of projects or experiments. He also controlled the telescope that was locked in its cabinet in Room 204A.

By now, Perry had outgrown this piece of school property—he had used the famous Mt. Wilson telescopes in California, and had access to very nice equipment at U. Rochester, through ASRAS. But it was nice that Mr. Subramanian offered. If he only knew!

Most people, outside of a few dedicated astrophysics scholars, had never heard of Frank Drake or his famous equation. Most people hated equations of any kind.

But this one was unique, and set in motion serious scientific inquiry into whether Life existed elsewhere in the Milky Way galaxy.

Perry was in the library quite a bit these days, once he got the go-ahead from the Science Department, who got the permission from the Principal. Perry would get the equivalent of three Science credits for this. He was pumped.

The library computers were fast, and the server connections were stable and reliable. Just what he needed. Browsing the Internet, he quickly came across a reference to Drake's equation. It wasn't about Math so much as it was about speculation in Astrobiology, a related field where people search for and predict some kind of Life out there in the stars.

Perry had a secret, a big secret. He already knew, or had reason to believe, that there were advanced cultures and civilizations that had crossed parsecs of space to come to visit our solar system.

He had photographic evidence—if not outright proof!

Margot, the resident Math champ, joined him at lunch one day.

"What is it you wanted to ask me, Perry?"

"Margot, take a look at this. Does the Drake Equation give us mathematical certainty that there are other intelligent species in Space?"

"Well, Perry, this so-called equation is not really one that can give us an answer. It's not like polynomials and quadratic functions, you see."

Perry didn't see, because equations with multiple variables was not taught in school until 9th or 10th Grade. Margot was considerably ahead of her fellow students on this one.

"The variables in Professor Drake's formula are too vast, too complex, to realistically calculate," Margot stated.

Perry looked at Margot. "Then it might surprise you that they have used the Drake Equation to estimate the number of potential civilizations in the Milky Way galaxy alone to be as many as 100 million! And the vast number of stars and planets orbiting them will be where we will find them."

"Really? That is incredible!"

"What Drake came to believe," Perry continued, "is that extraterrestrial civilizations are going to be a lot like ours—chatterboxes. They cannot keep silent, so they have to talk to someone, so they will send signals out into space in hopes that a sufficiently advanced culture can receive and decode them."

"Well let me know when you contact the aliens, Perry. I'm serious. I'm not mocking you. I know you too well to think you are an empty-headed dreamer. See you in Math class in third period."

Margot had Chinese parents, who immigrated to America for better opportunities for their children. But they were strict. Margot was expected to spend 80% of her time studying, with a focus on Mathematics. They told her Mathematics was the Queen of the Sciences, and a highway to success in the highly technical work environment in the Western world. And of course, they were right.

Margot sometimes complained about it and said she had no life, and why was she born to Asian parents, and so on.

But she conformed to her parents' wishes, and knew that post-graduate study at Harvard or Stanford were within her grasp. So she worked like a slave and got the kind of grades universities and colleges want to see.

The other 20% she spent with Perry and the gang at The Malt Shop, so she could give her eyeballs and brain a rest once in a while.

***

Perry had another secret. He secretly hoped he would hear from Macy, and have an excuse to see her, or at least have a conversation with her.

At night, when he lay his head on his pillow, he fantasized that he was older and taller, and could ask Macy out, and they could go ballroom dancing and he could touch her and hold her.

But Perry had a ways to go to manhood. He had, like, three hairs on his chin to shave, and he was completely in the dark about how to talk to girls, or what to talk about.

Girls spent most of the time talking. They asked permission of the teacher to go to the washroom and then met other girls to talk to there, or put on small dabs of lipstick or eyeliner. Stuff boys never learned to do and never would. Which made it a kind of pre-puberty fascination for guys.

When there was a substitute teacher, girls went out every five minutes, and the subs never remembered who had already gone, or for how many minutes. Whatever gossip was circulated in the Girls' washroom, it was theirs to know, and for boys to never find out.

So Perry waited at his laptop night after night for an e-mail from Macy that never seemed to come. He actually had real questions to ask. He knew about the Drake Equation for example, and was now researching about the Goldilocks Zone and what relationship to the Drake Equation it might have.

At least he was doing his Science thing, and preparing for university down the road. He had to control his emotions better, he realized. Time for girls later.

***

"Henry. Look at this." Perry's cell recorded an incoming call with fewer numbers than the normal 10-digit numbers. It was all 'ones' and 'zeroes'; binary code. It was a message maybe. But from whom?

"Spam," said Robert and Max.

"V-Mobile," said Margot and Rita.

"Wrong number," said Henry and Charmaine.

The next day it happened again. This time the numbers were repeated with each call. '886 000 000'; '886 000 000'; '886 000 000'.

"That sounds like a quantity," said Mr. Matson, the Science teacher for 7th and 8th grade classes at Brackendale.

"Like it measures something, and the sender wants us to figure out what that is?" Perry inquired.

"Maybe it's something we—meaning *you*— are supposed to know, Perry."

Perry was ready to beat his head on the desk.

"Henry? How far is it to Titan?"

"Lemme check. Ah, 4.2 billion kilometers."

"How many miles is that?"

"Ah...one sec...stupid calculator needs light to activate. Here it is: 886 million miles."

"Six zeroes—just like the coded message. Someone is telling us the precise distance to Saturn's biggest moon, Titan. The very moon which seems to have a mysterious nature of its own. Someone is trying to communicate with me, Henry."

A new message had appeared on the screen, while they were talking.

"Oh my gawd! Henry! Mr. Matson! Look at this number."

The screen showed just 4 characters this time: 204A. The number of the Science Lab at Brackendale, the number of the room they were in right now, at this very moment.

They all gasped and looked at each other.

"They know where you are, Perry," Mr. Matson said in a somber tone. "You can run, but you cannot hide."

"What do I do now? Call 'Ghostbusters'?"

Mr. Matson smiled and Henry fidgeting with his calculator.

"You'll have to deal with them, I guess, Perry. This is one of those moments that only a few are chosen to experience. You have a mission to fulfill, and they seem to want to help you."

"Oh sure, Mr. Matson. Like have Men In Black stalk me, phone hackers text me, flying saucers zap my friends." *Oops. Forgot to avoid mentioning Mike's traumatic encounter in Tesla Park.*

"What do you mean, Perry? Someone had contact with actual aliens, someone you *know*?" Mr. Matson closed the hall door and locked it, which he never did.

Perry quickly sketched the events of the last month and a half for his teacher. Mr. Matson was someone you could absolutely trust, not only because he knew everything about Science, but because he was someone who would never ever betray you. He was what Perry's grandfather would call a 'standup guy'.

"You had better keep quiet about this, Perry," Mr. Matson said.

"That's just what everybody tells me: don't talk, keep silent, they'll be trouble.

I am getting frustrated with all the secrecy about something many people believe is real, and if it is—*if*—then we, as scientists, have an ethical duty to speak up and demand there is an investigation that includes the public."

"You're quite right, Perry, and I sympathize with your position. However, at the very least, we should proceed with caution."

A key fiddled in the lock and the door opened, and Mr. Subramanian came in to prepare for class.

"As I was saying, Perry, your research is good but still needs improvement. Why don't you go to the library downtown after school, and see what you can dig up?"

Mr. Matson was giving Perry and Henry an opening to scoot out the door, without any awkward questions about why they were there, and what they were discussing.

"That was close," Henry said.

"Sure was," said Perry.

Just then Perry noticed he had one voice message. Fervently hoping it might be Macy Lawrence, he punched into his PIN code and pressed '1' to hear new messages.

But it wasn't Macy. It was an odd, metallic voice that said: "Your product will be shipped to you soon." *Click.* End of call.

"I didn't order anything, Henry. What is going on?"

"I don't know, Perry, but I *do* know if we are late for The Crusher's Math class, we are going to get chewed out, like always. I would rather avoid that."

"Let's go," Perry urged. It was Third Period. The one everyone dreaded.

CHAPTER ELEVEN   THE GOLDILOCKS ZONE

Modern astronomers, using the most advanced technology, are on a quest to find life out in the vast ocean of stars we call the Universe. Ever since Frank Drake and Carl Sagan and others started seriously looking, scientists have been obsessed with finding exoplanets in what they call The Goldilocks Zone.

This refers to areas around suitable stars that may have habitable planets. That means, other forms of Life will develop, and perhaps will contact us one day.

"Why do they call them 'Goldilocks Planets', Perry?" Henry was curious.

"Remember the children's story about Goldilocks and the Three Bears? Lost in the woods, this girl Goldilocks let herself into their house. Then she ate their breakfast and slept in their beds, until they discovered her, and kicked her out. Pretty funny when you think of it.

Anyhow, her way of determining if the porridge was okay to eat was to taste all three bowls. Her conclusion was that one was too hot, one was too cold, but the last one was just right. So scientists say that we will find lots of planets that are too close to the star and are too hot, or too far from the parent star, so are too cold, but--- there just may be one that is 'just right' in terms of temperature, and chemicals that give rise to living organisms."

"Like nitrogen and carbon."

"Exactly, Henry. We have instruments that can analyze light from distant stars and see if those elements are present, or not. That is one of the ways we find worlds in The Goldilocks Zone." Every astronomer agrees that there is Life waiting to be discovered; they even have new branches of Science like Exobiology. What possibilities we have, Henry!"

***

School was over for the day, so the gang headed off to The Malt Shop, which offered hot cocoa instead of ice-cream, because it was winter. The windows were decorated with light-up Santas, and ribbons, and Christmas decorations. Students were trying to guess what they would get for Christmas.

"I get a new mountain bike, I bet!" crowed Robert.

"I get a new i-Phone I hope," said Margot.

"I just want to be left alone to sleep," Charmaine said.

Everyone agreed that sleep was the best.

"What do you want, Perry?" said Margot and Max.

"A new telescope would be nice; my old one is kinda scratched on the lenses."

Randy the Gorilla leaned out and mentioned that he always gets socks. He's got so many socks from all the Christmases that he could open a clothing store.

"I'll get you something, Randy," said Charmaine, who was the only girl in 8th Grade that would talk to Randy publicly. She said he was 'a teddy bear'. Not to his face, though.

"One day I want to try skiing," Perry said. "It looks like so much fun and we get lots of snow so why waste it?"

Christmas was still two weeks away so there was another week of suffering at school, and then time off for Winter Break and holiday parties for every school and business. The forecast called for snow, so that would make it a White Christmas. There had already been three inches over the last two nights, and the magic of streetlamps and colored lights strung on trees and rooftops gave an air of festivity to Brackendale.

***

So it was a very curious thing that a large package had been delivered to Number 9, Galileo Court, to Perry's house, fourteen days before Christmas. Whatever it was, it was too big to put under any Christmas tree. Henry was the first to notice.

"Hey, there is no name or address on the front of the box."

"Neither are there any footprints in the snow, or tire tracks, to indicate who left it."

"I get a funny feeling this is for you, Perry."

"Help me lift it, Henry. Gosh, it must weigh nearly forty pounds. I haven't carried that much since we snitched the telescope from the school."

Perry fished the front door key from under the mat and swung the door open. Duke came bounding up and sniffed the box, then retreated to the kitchen.

"Let's haul it downstairs, Henry. We can open it there without leaving a mess."

Perry went down the stairs backwards and they parked the cardboard container on the concrete floor near the washing machine.

"Let me get a knife. There. Let's open it, Henry."

"Shouldn't we wait for Christmas, or something? We could ask your folks."

"How do we know what it is? It might have been delivered to the wrong house and we have to get it to the right house in time for Christmas." Perry was slitting the corners and peeling back the silver duct tape holding it together.

There was no address on the front, no return address or name of the sender, nothing!

Perry gasped at what he saw.

"A reflector, a 12-inch Newtonian reflector, Henry! I sure hope this is not a misdirected package. I hope the real owner doesn't show up on Christmas Day and ask where his package is. Can you believe it, Henry?"

There were no marking or brand logos or anything on the sleek black instrument. There was a base with a remarkable smooth motion as it swiveled easily back and forth.

"This is nice!" said Henry. "This is really what we need, Perry. The Geminid and Lyrid meteor showers are about to commence, and we can get a pretty good view of them with this."

"Perry?" Henry looked up at his friend standing stiff as a pole, with a small card in his hand. "What is it, Perry?"

Perry handed the card to Henry. It was a full-color photograph in high resolution of the moon Titan. It had the dense clouds, and the yellow-blue features of the surface that had only been released by NASA this past summer.

On the back were written these words: *Keep watching, Perry. You are not alone.*

"Are you going to tell your parents about this?"

"Not right now, Henry, not until I figure out what this all means.

Mystery codes on my phone, gifts at my door. Notice that it wasn't me the MIBs visited, and it wasn't me that the saucer beamed up. Someone is watching over me, Henry. Gotta be! But why? Why are they showing me that they are real, and at the same time, protecting me?"

"Beats me, Perry."

"Henry? Do you think I am 'special'? I mean, am I being chosen for a unique mission or something?"

"If I were an alien scout, I'd choose you just because you know everything about this planet and would be a real asset to their program. If they wanted to colonize Earth, they would choose someone like you, Perry. Know what I mean?"

"Quick! Back in the box. My Mom's home, with Gabby."

The Doberman barked its excited 'welcome home' to his family. That gave the boys time to stash the box in the laundry room, behind the hot water heater.

"Perry? Are you home, honey?"

"Yes, Mom, Henry and I are just watching cartoons on TV."

"Ask Henry if he'd like to stay for dinner."

"Henry? Would you care to be our guest at our evening meal tonight?" Perry dropped his voice like he was a pirate, or Robin Hood.

"Why yes, Sir Perry, I would be honored." Henry smiled, and Perry winked. The box would remain under wraps for the time being.

Chapter Twelve   Pennies From Heaven

The e-mail that Perry had been waiting for finally arrived. It was from Macy.

> From: **Macy L** <MUFONnychap>
>
> Subject: Meeting this week
>
> Date: December 7, 2017
>
> To: Perry Normal

Hey, Perry! How is the skywatching going? Our upstate New York Chapter of MUFON is meeting this week. Any way you could make it? It would be great to see you! Or you could log in to the meeting on Skype. Let me know.

Macy ☺

Perry wanted desperately to go to this meeting, perhaps to see Macy again, or perhaps to see what this legendary UFO investigation organization had to say about the skies of New York.

But who to ask? He thought about Henry. Would his parents drive them all the way to Rochester for a three hour meeting with a bunch of UFO enthusiasts? Only one way to find out.

"Henry. Text me. Important."

Henry did.

"Ask your parents if they would like to do a little Christmas shopping in Rochester."

Henry decided to call instead.

"What's going on, Perry?"

"Macy Lawrence invited us—well, me, but I'm sure you are welcome, to the next meeting of the local chapter of MUFON. We don't have a chance unless we get a ride. Can you ask your Dad?"

"Ok, wait." Henry put the phone down and could be heard speaking with someone in the background.

"We're in, Perry. Ever since Dad saw those Men in Black on our doorstep, he's become interested in UFO phenomena and paranormal stuff. Isn't that weird? He never was before!

Anyway, what evening and what time?"

Perry and Henry were ready. Henry's Dad was an electrical engineer and worked for New York State Electric and Gas as a technology consultant and troubleshooter. He had a big SUV that was perfect for the highway in any weather, and Perry's parents were comfortable with Peter Schuyler driving their son. They didn't know the Schuylers that well but they liked Henry and knew he was Perry's all-time best friend.

"I drive this road a lot, you know," Mr. Schuyler was chatting with the boys as they headed onto the freeway south to Rochester, about an hour's drive from home.

"I know it like the back of my hand!" He drove fast, and he knew all the places where there were speed-traps where state troopers lurked to catch speeders.

The meeting was being held at U. Rochester campus, in the Science Wing. There was a bigger group than Perry expected.

The speaker was a young man with a beard and glasses who looked unsettled about something. He stepped up to the mic and cleared his throat loudly, which meant for everyone to quieten down.

Brackendale's principal did the same thing at assemblies.

"Welcome everyone, and a special welcome to newcomers. We have a lot to cover so I will get right to the first item on our agenda."

Henry and Perry were bored already with all the meeting talk. Henry's Dad was gazing around; he whispered that he hoped no one would recognize him.

"First of all, thanks to all our fieldworkers— especially Macy Lawrence—who has been gathering information from all the reports coming in about fireballs, and bright lights all over the state.

What we think you should know is that UFO sightings have increased dramatically in the last several months. We don't know why.

The Air Force denies knowing what these objects are, and are very quiet about their own programs to develop stealth aircraft and others that use alleged alien technology such as anti-gravity propulsion systems."

A hand shot up in the audience and the speaker paused to let the man speak.

"I'm an officer in the Air Force, sonny, and if we have secret missions, that means it's none of your damn business, so leave the Air Force out of this."

Suddenly a dozen hands were raised, and the level of chatter got louder.

"What about the secret Space Command, then? Why doesn't the Air Force, or the Pentagon tell us what's going on? We are not blind. We see them, we video them with our cell phones and cameras. We know they are there," one man shouted.

A lady in the back stood up. She had a booming voice.

"We have a Constitutional right to freedom of information and freedom of speech. That is why this organization exists—to find the truth and let the people of the United States know just what is happening."

The crowd started talking, like a million bees all swarming around their hive.

"All right, settle down people. No one is denying our rights. We have a petition to the President that is going out; you can sign it by the door on your way out tonight. Now let me get back to what I was saying."

Henry and his Dad were smiling and thoroughly enjoying this, like they were at a baseball game or something.

Perry was trying to spot Macy. He just wanted to be alone with her for two minutes, just to chat and say whatever.

He saw her.

She was saying something into the ear of the speaker, who nodded and wrote something down. She was in the front row, so Perry could not get to her.

"Ahem," the speaker said. "There seems to evidence that the upswing in earthquakes and natural disasters of all kinds correlates with the uptick in UFO sightings worldwide. Many have been seen near volcanoes, or sites of earthquake activity. Others have been seen close to military installations, or observing military exercises by American forces, and by others not so friendly to American interests."

"What does he mean 'American interests', Dad?" Henry said.

"He means that our country is doing business abroad, and is involved in intense political situations with nations that don't want to be our friend or help us bring peace and democracy to the world. So our ambassadors, and our large corporations like the oil companies, are having a tough time in particular places on the globe." Henry looked at Perry and shrugged.

Adults know all this political stuff, but it's totally boring to us, Perry was thinking to himself. He winked at Henry.

"So," the speaker went on, " let us be vigilant, keep sending us your photos and reports of 'close encounters' so we have proof of what we say is going on. It should be noted that the U.K. recently released formerly secret files on UFO activity in Britain and there is absolutely no doubt it is real, and the British government knows that."

The chattering started again as people took in this new information.

"Ah, attention please. I have a special announcement." He leaned down and said loud enough for the mic to pick up: "Macy, could you come up now?"

Macy smiled broadly as she stepped up to the podium.

"Thank you, Jamie. I want to introduce a special young member of ASRAS and of MUFON New York who has been doing some stargazing for NASA/JPL and is going to be recognized for his contribution to astronomy and the study of Space."

Then the unbelievable happened!

She pointed her upturned hand right at Perry, and said, "Perry, will you please come up?"

"Ladies and gentleman, Perry Normal from Brackendale Middle School. He has contributed to the discovery and study of Planet X, and helped prove that it is part of our solar system, a part we did not know was even there. Congratulations, Perry!"

The applause was thunderous. Perry blushed. Everyone looked at him. Macy hugged him. He pulled the microphone arm down a bit so he could be heard.

"Um, thank you very much. Thank you, Macy. I didn't know that my summer research would matter to anybody. In fact, the military seemed to think I was nuts, and tried to hush me up.
I started suspecting something when I did my first investigations when Henry and I took the Science telescope home, without telling anyone."

The audience laughed.

"But we returned it later…"

And so Perry gave an account of how he came to believe that a huge new planet had arrived from somewhere in Space, and why he needed to tell somebody.

"I want to share this moment with my best friend, Henry Schuyler. Come up please, Henry." People were clapping like mad.

Henry stood shyly beside Perry in the spotlight. Suddenly flashes from cameras and cell phones started popping, and Macy joined them for the local news photo-op.

On the way home, Henry's Dad couldn't stop jabbering; Perry thought that this is where Henry gets his tendency to talk without stopping when he gets excited. *It's hereditary.*

What was in Perry's mind, though, was the special sweetness of having a hug with someone you have a crush on, but can never tell them.

***

It was the last Science class of the Fall Term. Mr. Matson brought in the DVD movie *Contact* with

Jodie Foster for the class to watch. A small reward for a hard semester. It was about first contact with an extraterrestrial civilization on another star. It was based on a book by Carl Sagan, the spokesman for SETI and the whole movement for finding extraterrestrial civilizations.

That gave Mr. Matson time to call Perry into his office for a little chat.

"Am I in trouble?" Perry said. He was getting used to being a target since his summer fiasco.

"No, no, nothing like that. Quite the opposite, Perry. I want you to read this article, that I think might interest you."

Mr. Matson had copies of *Astronomy Today,* and *Sky & Telescope* magazine. The cover was attention-getting! It was a monstrous shadow, with stars in behind, and tiny Pluto in the foreground. The shape suggested it was a giant spherical object moving toward our solar system.

It said NASA had discovered a new planet at the edge of our solar system that was as large as Jupiter, and matched the description of the mystery Planet X. The conspiracy theories were correct, it said, but more research had to be done on the significance of this amazing discovery.

"That means you were right, Perry!"

"Why are they telling us *now*? They made us keep it hush-hush and threatened us. Now they act like they knew it was here all along and it was never going to crash into the Earth anyway."

Perry's temper began to flare, and he got to his feet and started pacing the floor.

"Maybe they realized that if kids like you could detect these unusual phenomena in space, then their secret was going to come out, then their cover was blown."

"Here. I want to show you *this*." He reached into the drawer of his desk.

It was a certificate, in a nice gold frame. It said:

This is to recognize the Science Department at Brackendale Middle School, Brackendale, New York, for its contribution to Astronomical Science and our National Space Program.

The NASA logo was in the corner, and it was signed by the head scientist at JPL in Pasadena, California.

"So that means the government isn't after me anymore?"

"Yeah, Perry. You are a free man again."

Perry Normal, Junior Scientist, head of the Science and Astronomy Club at Brackendale Middle School, member of ASRAS, MUFON, and the American Meteor Society, was free to watch the skies as he pleased.

Free to do what he did best—take Science as far as it could go.

The End

Read more of Perry's astonishing exploits by contacting the publisher and ordering them.

Red Pine Publishing

100 Earlsdale Ave., York, Ontario M6C 1L3 Canada

or at:

myredpine@gmail.com   Order Dept.

Author profile found on Amazon.com/books under the author's name: Mason Stone.

www.ingramcontent.com/pod-product-compliance
Lightning Source LLC
Chambersburg PA
CBHW071120100726
47908CB00008B/2435